J
Pe
Van . . . . Part one

$10.99
ocn515477542
12/01/2010

NANCY DREW

THE NEW CASE FILES

Based on the series by Carolyn Keene

Girl Detective®

VAMPIRE SLAYER

PART ONE

By Petrucha, Kinney & Murase

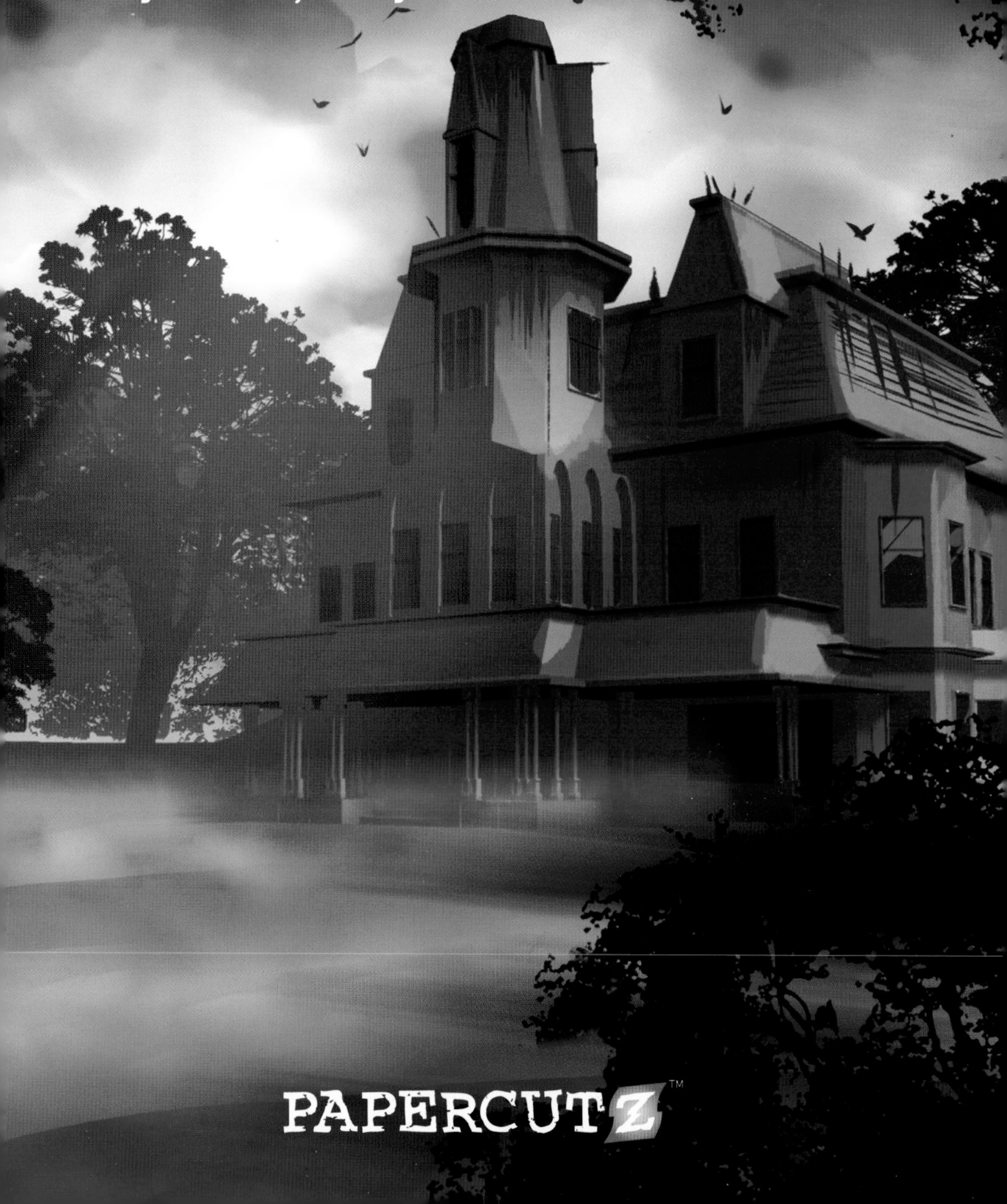

PAPERCUTZ™

NANCY DREW GRAPHIC NOVELS AVAILABLE FROM PAPERCUTZ

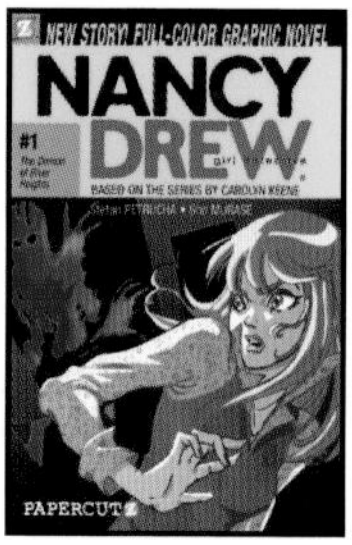
NEW STORY! FULL-COLOR GRAPHIC NOVEL
NANCY
DREW
#1
BASED ON THE SERIES BY CAROLYN KEENE
PAPERCUTZ

#1 “The Demon of River Heights”

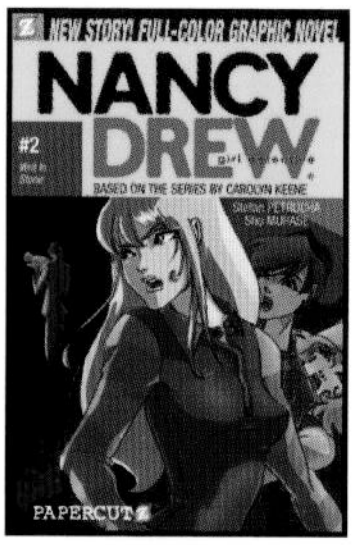
NEW STORY! FULL-COLOR GRAPHIC NOVEL
NANCY
DREW
#2
BASED ON THE SERIES BY CAROLYN KEENE
PAPERCUTZ

#2 “Writ In Stone”

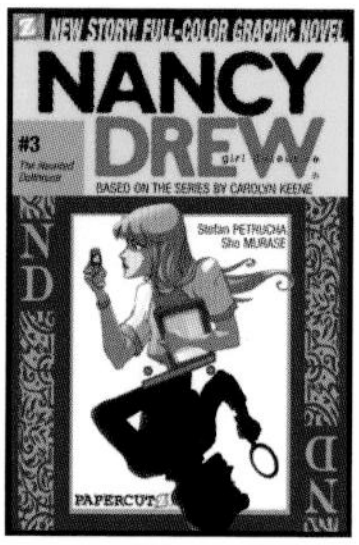
NEW STORY! FULL-COLOR GRAPHIC NOVEL
NANCY
DREW
#3
BASED ON THE SERIES BY CAROLYN KEENE
Stefan PETRUCHA
Sho MURASE
PAPERCUTZ

#3 “The Haunted Dollhouse"

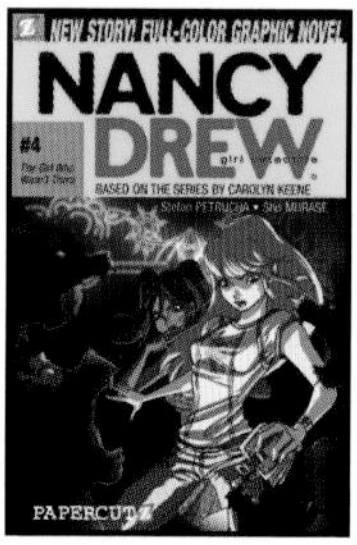
NEW STORY! FULL-COLOR GRAPHIC NOVEL
NANCY
DREW
#4
BASED ON THE SERIES BY CAROLYN KEENE
PAPERCUTZ

#4 “The Girl Who Wasn't There"

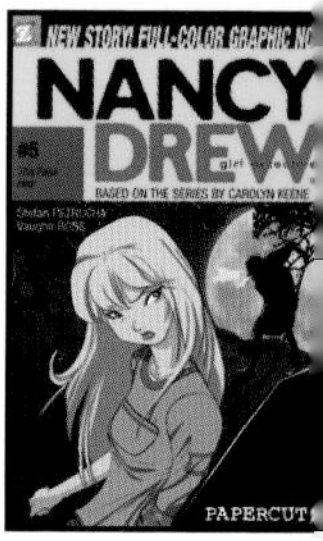
NEW STORY! FULL-COLOR GRAPHIC NOVEL
NANCY
DREW
#5
BASED ON THE SERIES BY CAROLYN KEENE
PAPERCUTZ

#5 “The Fake Heir”

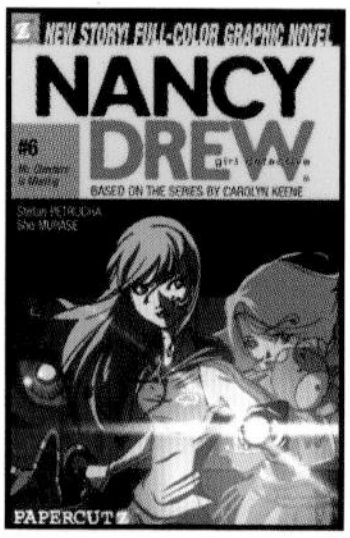
NEW STORY! FULL-COLOR GRAPHIC NOVEL
NANCY
DREW
#6
BASED ON THE SERIES BY CAROLYN KEENE
PAPERCUTZ

#6 “Mr. Cheeters Is Missing”

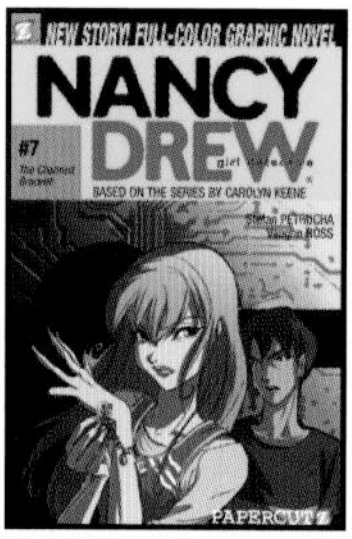
NEW STORY! FULL-COLOR GRAPHIC NOVEL
NANCY
DREW
#7
BASED ON THE SERIES BY CAROLYN KEENE
PAPERCUTZ

#7 “The Charmed Bracelet"

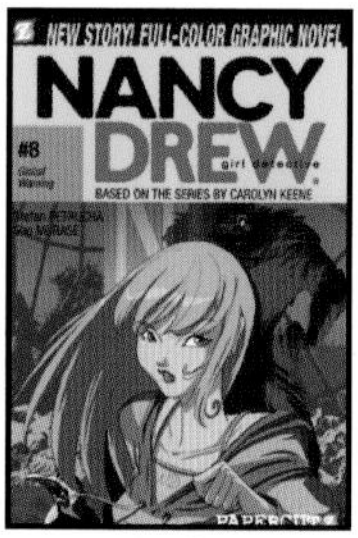
NEW STORY! FULL-COLOR GRAPHIC NOVEL
NANCY
DREW
#8
BASED ON THE SERIES BY CAROLYN KEENE

#8 “Global Warning"

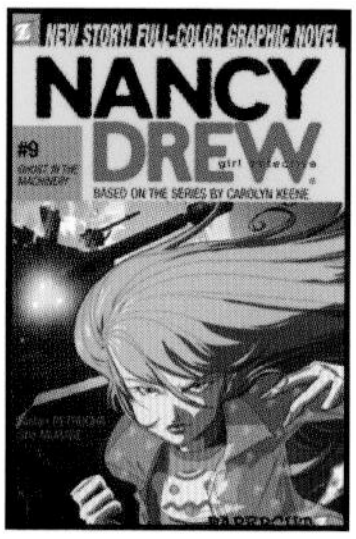
NEW STORY! FULL-COLOR GRAPHIC NOVEL
NANCY
DREW
#9
BASED ON THE SERIES BY CAROLYN KEENE

#9 “Ghost In The Machinery"

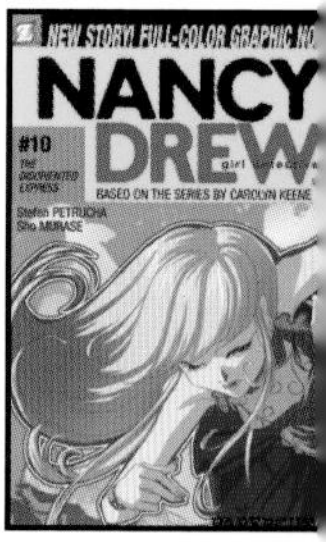
NEW STORY! FULL-COLOR GRAPHIC NOVEL
NANCY
DREW
#10
BASED ON THE SERIES BY CAROLYN KEENE

#10 “The Disorier ed Express"

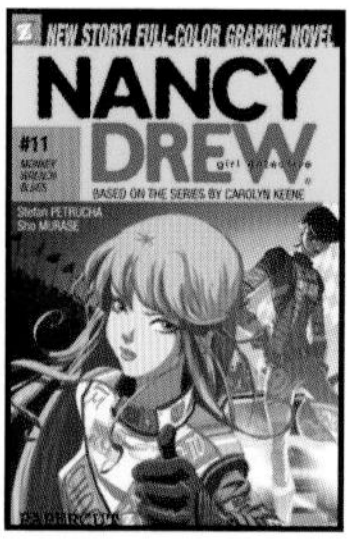
NEW STORY! FULL-COLOR GRAPHIC NOVEL
NANCY
DREW
#11
BASED ON THE SERIES BY CAROLYN KEENE
PAPERCUTZ

#11 “Monkey Wrench Blues"

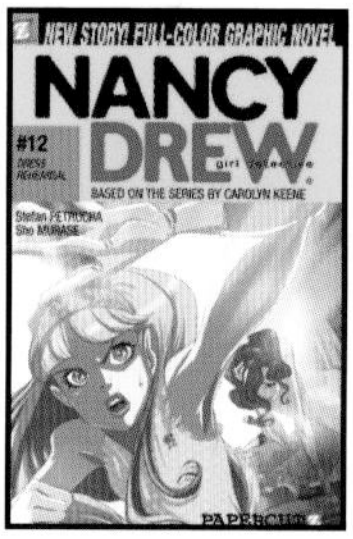
NEW STORY! FULL-COLOR GRAPHIC NOVEL
NANCY
DREW
#12
BASED ON THE SERIES BY CAROLYN KEENE
PAPERCUTZ

#12 “Dress Reversal"

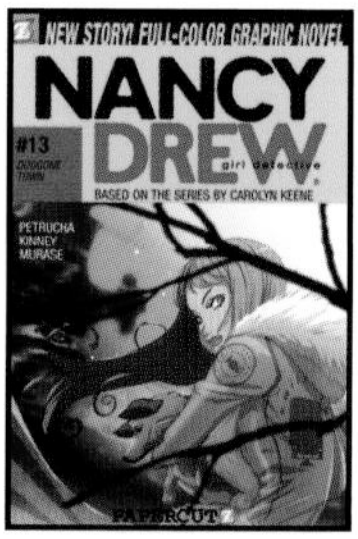
NEW STORY! FULL-COLOR GRAPHIC NOVEL
NANCY
DREW
#13
BASED ON THE SERIES BY CAROLYN KEENE
PAPERCUTZ

#13 “Doggone Town”

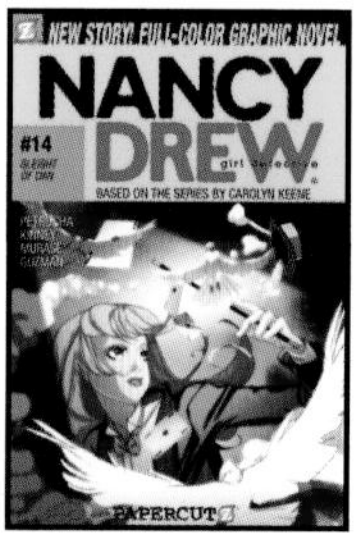
NEW STORY! FULL-COLOR GRAPHIC NOVEL
NANCY
DREW
#14
BASED ON THE SERIES BY CAROLYN KEENE
PAPERCUTZ

#14 “Sleight of Dan”

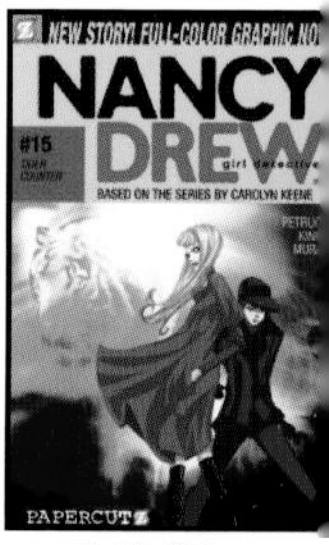
NEW STORY! FULL-COLOR GRAPHIC NOVEL
NANCY
DREW
#15
BASED ON THE SERIES BY CAROLYN KEENE
PAPERCUTZ

#15 “Tiger Counter”

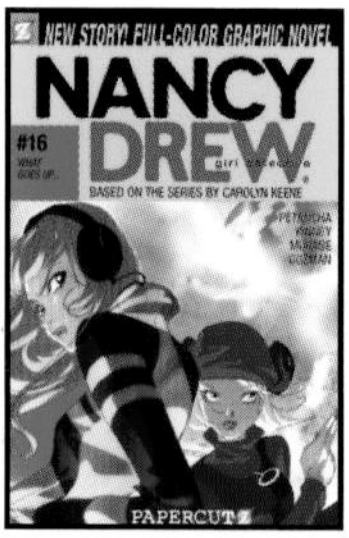
NEW STORY! FULL-COLOR GRAPHIC NOVEL
NANCY
DREW
#16
BASED ON THE SERIES BY CAROLYN KEENE
PAPERCUTZ

#16 “What Goes Up...”

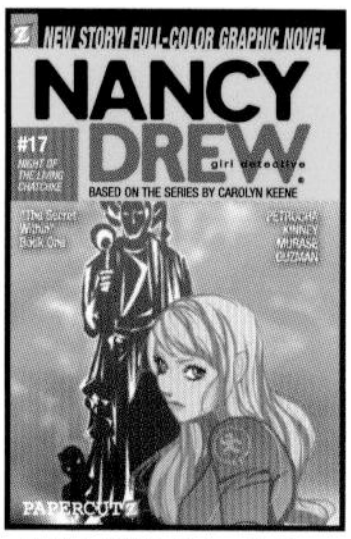
NEW STORY! FULL-COLOR GRAPHIC NOVEL
NANCY
DREW
#17
BASED ON THE SERIES BY CAROLYN KEENE
PAPERCUTZ

#17 “Night of the Living Chatchke”

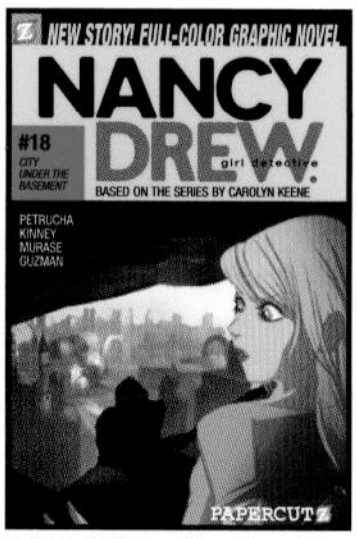
NEW STORY! FULL-COLOR GRAPHIC NOVEL
NANCY
DREW
#18
BASED ON THE SERIES BY CAROLYN KEENE
PETRUCHA
KINNEY
MURASE
GUZMAN
PAPERCUTZ

#18 “City Under the Basement”

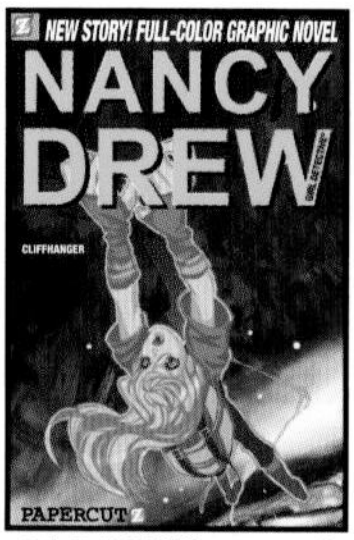
NEW STORY! FULL-COLOR GRAPHIC NOVEL
NANCY
DREW
CLIFFHANGER
PAPERCUTZ

#19 “Cliffhanger”

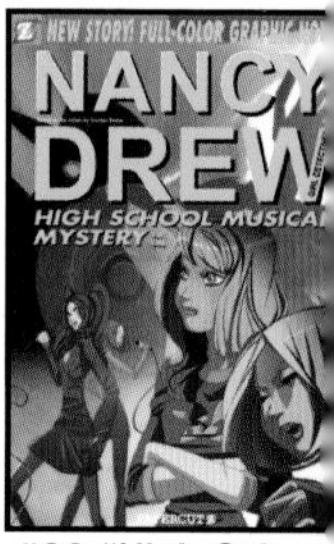
NANCY
DREW
HIGH SCHOOL MUSICAL MYSTERY

#20 “High Schoo Musical Mystery’

Graphic Novels #1-19 are $7.95 each in paperback, $12.95 hardcover. Graphic Novel #20 is $8.99 in paperback, $13.99 hardcover. Please add $4.00 for postage and handling for the first book, add $1.00 for each additional book. Please make check payable to NBM Publishing. Send to:

Papercutz, 40 Exchange Place, Suite 1308, New York, NY 10005, 1-800-886-1223

www.papercutz.com

NANCY DREW

THE NEW CASE FILES

Based on the series by Carolyn Keene — Girl Detective®

VAMPIRE SLAYER PART ONE

STEFAN PETRUCHA & SARAH KINNEY • Writers
SHO MURASE • Artist
with 3D CG elements and color by CARLOS JOSE GUZMAN
Based on the series by
CAROLYN KEENE

PAPERCUTZ™
New York

Let me introduce myself. Or did I already? No, probably not—at least not so you'd recognize me. I'm Nancy Drew. My friends call me Nancy. My enemies call me a lot of other things, like "that girl who cooked my goose." They actually sometimes speak like that, but what can you expect from criminals? See, I'm a detective. Not really. I mean, I don't have a license or anything. I don't carry a gun (not that I would touch one of those even if I could) or a badge. I'm not even old enough to have one. But I am old enough to know when something isn't right, when somebody's getting an unfair deal, or when someone's done something they shouldn't do. And I know how to stop them, catch them, and get them into the hands of the law, where they belong. I take those things seriously and I'm almost never wrong.

Not that my best friends Bess and George would agree with that. They tell me I'm wrong a lot, and they have to cover for me all the time just to make me look good. I think that's what best friends do for one another. Bess would tell you I dress badly. I call it casual. George would tell you I'm not focused. By that she'd mean that once again I forgot to fill my car with gas or bring enough money to buy lunch. I'm always focused when it comes to crime. Always.

"Vampire Slayer" Part One
STEFAN PETRUCHA & SARAH KINNEY – Writers
SHO MURASE — Artist
with 3D CG elements and color by CARLOS JOSE GUZMAN
BRYAN SENKA – Letterer
TROY HAHN – Production
MICHAEL PETRANEK – Editorial Assistant
JIM SALICRUP
Editor-in-Chief

ISBN: 978-1-59707-213-7 paperback edition
ISBN: 978-1-59707-214-4 hardcover edition

Printed in China
July 2010 by Asia One Printing LTD.
13/F Asia One Tower
8 Fung Yip St., Chaiwan
Hong Kong

Distributed by Macmillan.

First Printing

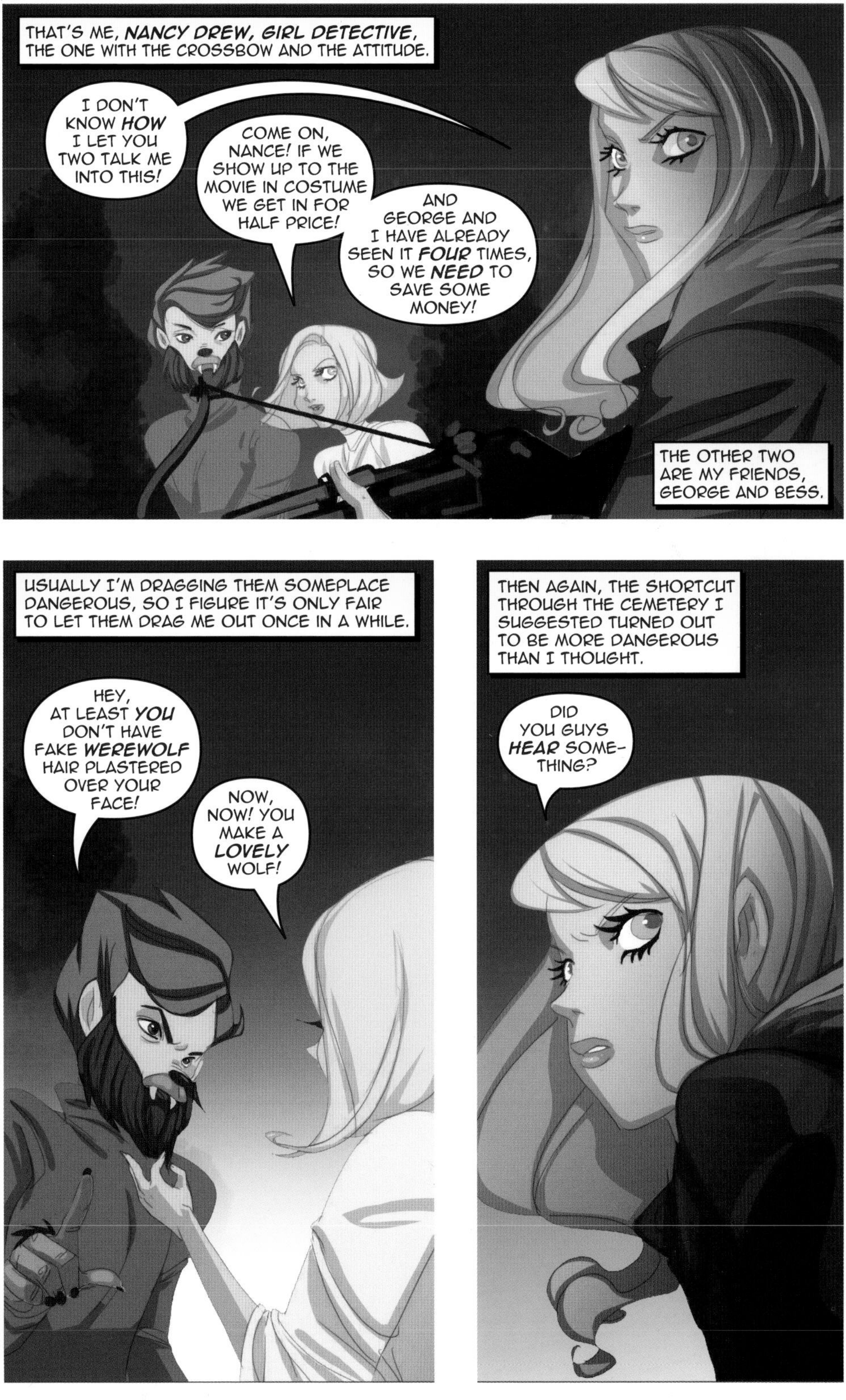
THAT'S ME, NANCY DREW, GIRL DETECTIVE, THE ONE WITH THE CROSSBOW AND THE ATTITUDE.
I DON'T KNOW HOW I LET YOU TWO TALK ME INTO THIS!
COME ON, NANCE! IF WE SHOW UP TO THE MOVIE IN COSTUME WE GET IN FOR HALF PRICE!
AND GEORGE AND I HAVE ALREADY SEEN IT FOUR TIMES, SO WE NEED TO SAVE SOME MONEY!
THE OTHER TWO ARE MY FRIENDS, GEORGE AND BESS.
USUALLY I'M DRAGGING THEM SOMEPLACE DANGEROUS, SO I FIGURE IT'S ONLY FAIR TO LET THEM DRAG ME OUT ONCE IN A WHILE.
HEY, AT LEAST YOU DON'T HAVE FAKE WEREWOLF HAIR PLASTERED OVER YOUR FACE!
NOW, NOW! YOU MAKE A LOVELY WOLF!
THEN AGAIN, THE SHORTCUT THROUGH THE CEMETERY I SUGGESTED TURNED OUT TO BE MORE DANGEROUS THAN I THOUGHT.
DID YOU GUYS HEAR SOME-THING?

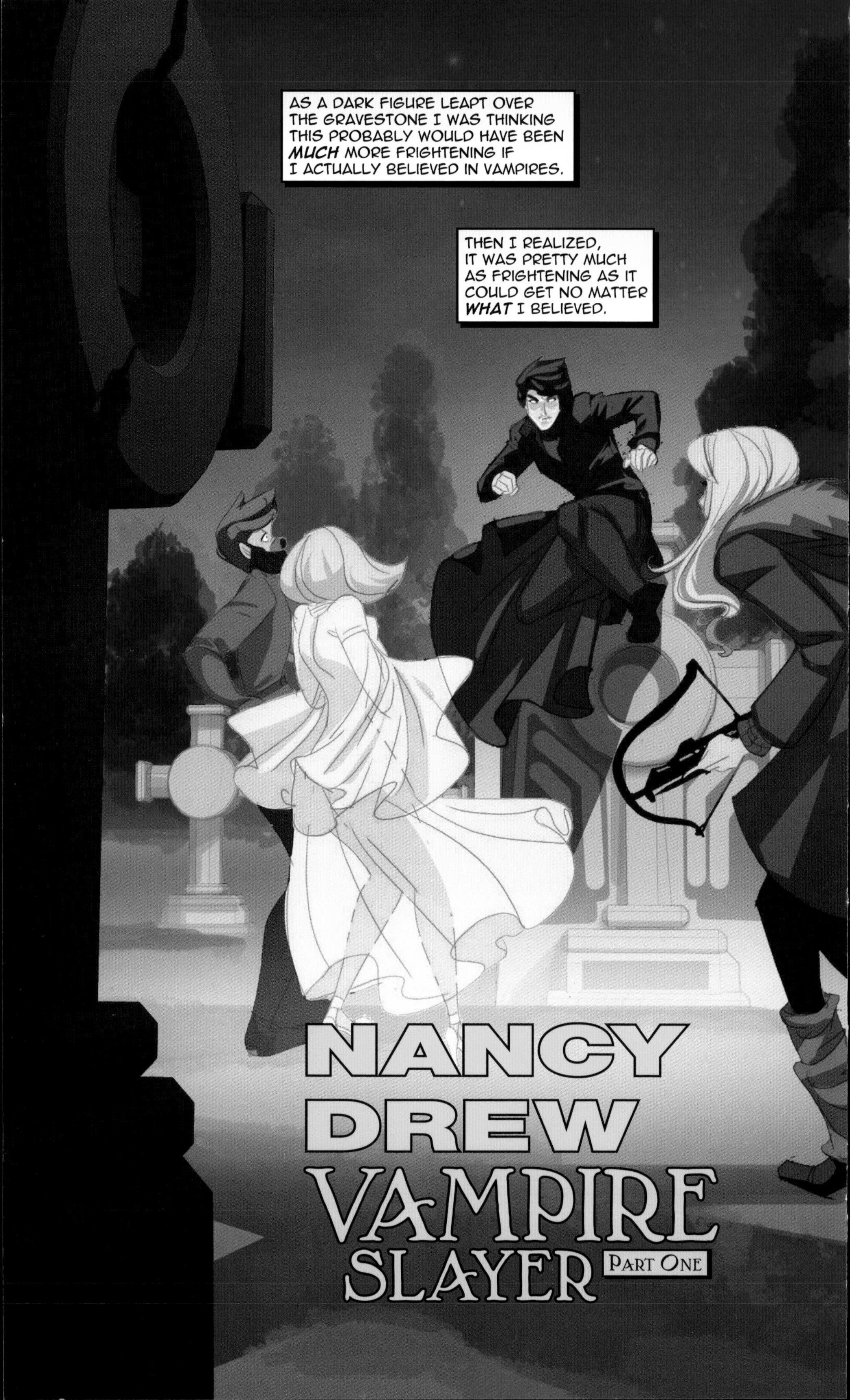
AS A DARK FIGURE LEAPT OVER THE GRAVESTONE I WAS THINKING THIS PROBABLY WOULD HAVE BEEN *MUCH* MORE FRIGHTENING IF I ACTUALLY BELIEVED IN VAMPIRES.
THEN I REALIZED, IT WAS PRETTY MUCH AS FRIGHTENING AS IT COULD GET NO MATTER *WHAT* I BELIEVED.
NANCY DREW
VAMPIRE SLAYER
PART ONE

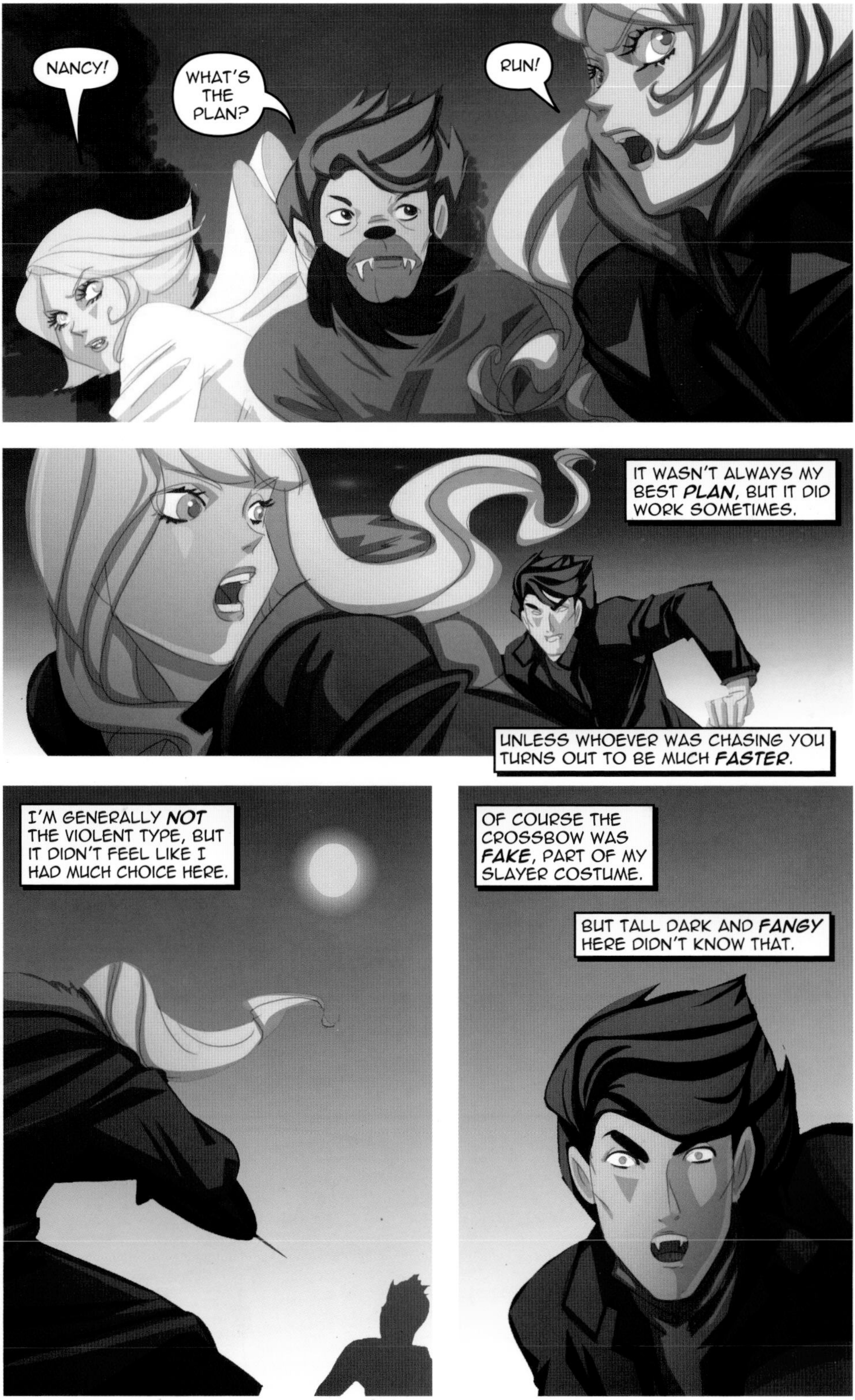
NANCY!
WHAT'S THE PLAN?
RUN!
IT WASN'T ALWAYS MY BEST PLAN, BUT IT DID WORK SOMETIMES.
UNLESS WHOEVER WAS CHASING YOU TURNS OUT TO BE MUCH FASTER.
I'M GENERALLY NOT THE VIOLENT TYPE, BUT IT DIDN'T FEEL LIKE I HAD MUCH CHOICE HERE.
OF COURSE THE CROSSBOW WAS FAKE, PART OF MY SLAYER COSTUME.
BUT TALL DARK AND FANGY HERE DIDN'T KNOW THAT.

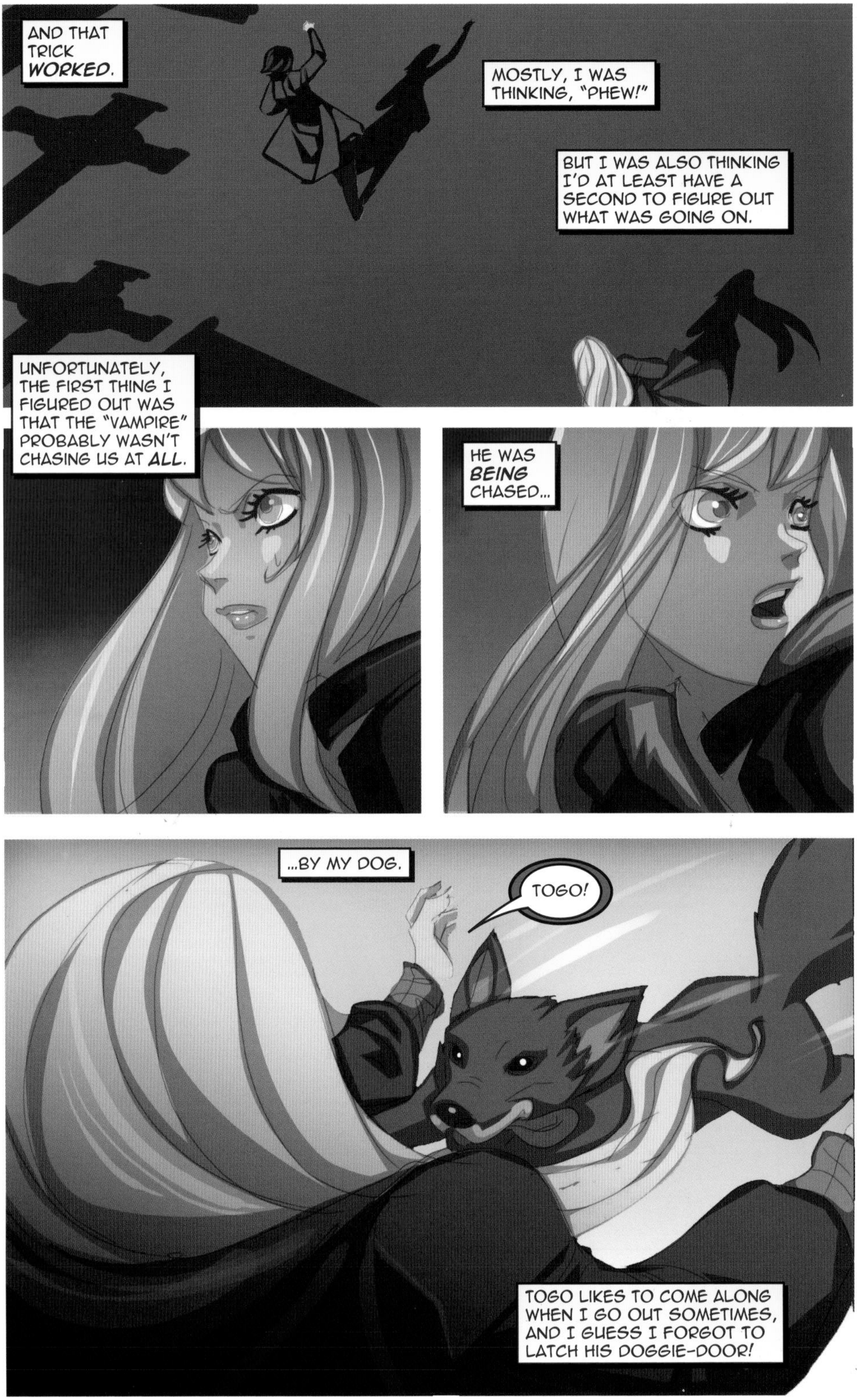
AND THAT TRICK WORKED.
MOSTLY, I WAS THINKING, "PHEW!"
BUT I WAS ALSO THINKING I'D AT LEAST HAVE A SECOND TO FIGURE OUT WHAT WAS GOING ON.
UNFORTUNATELY, THE FIRST THING I FIGURED OUT WAS THAT THE "VAMPIRE" PROBABLY WASN'T CHASING US AT ALL.
HE WAS BEING CHASED...
...BY MY DOG.
TOGO!
TOGO LIKES TO COME ALONG WHEN I GO OUT SOMETIMES, AND I GUESS I FORGOT TO LATCH HIS DOGGIE-DOOR!

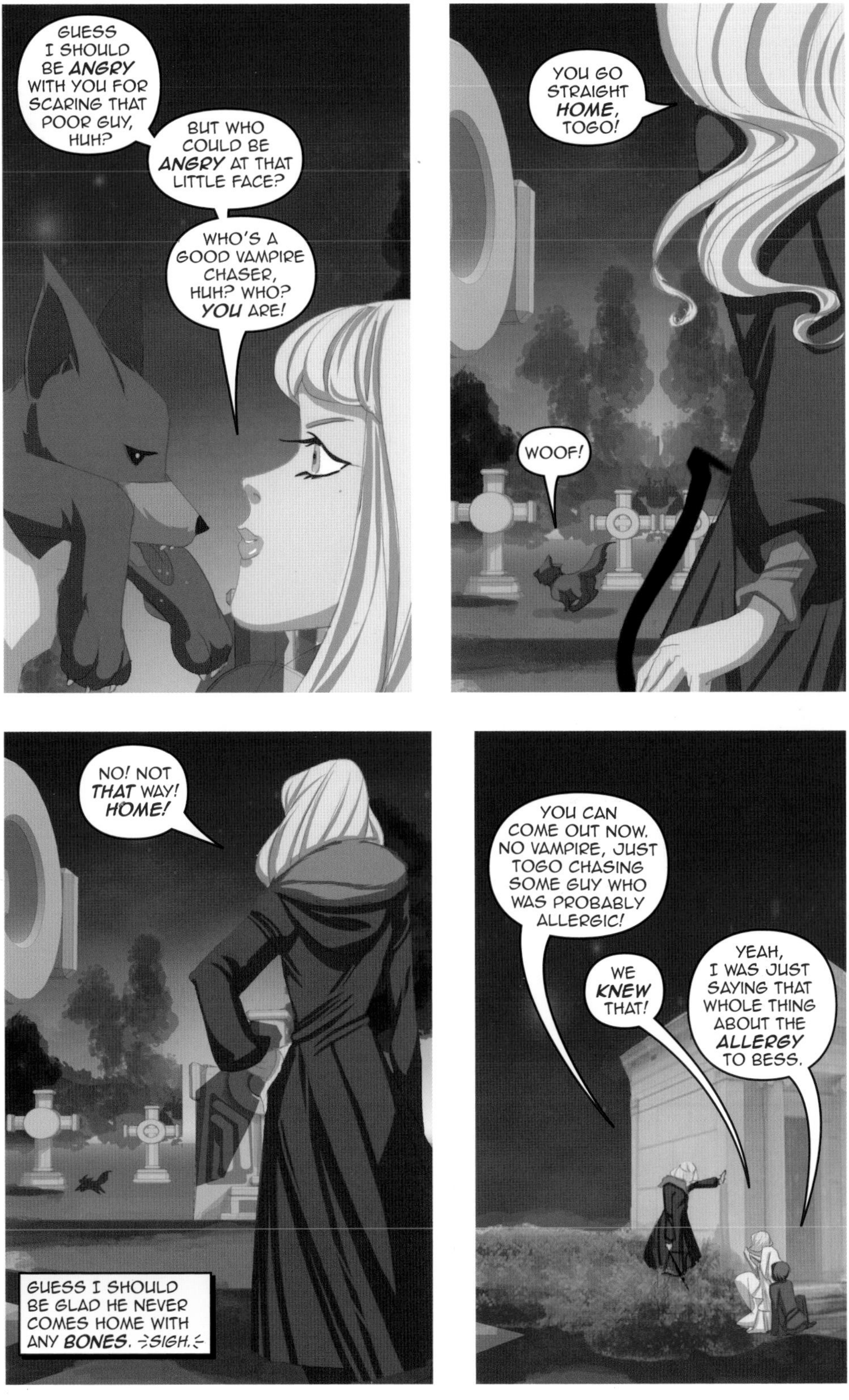
GUESS I SHOULD BE ANGRY WITH YOU FOR SCARING THAT POOR GUY, HUH?
BUT WHO COULD BE ANGRY AT THAT LITTLE FACE?
WHO'S A GOOD VAMPIRE CHASER, HUH? WHO? YOU ARE!
YOU GO STRAIGHT HOME, TOGO!
WOOF!
NO! NOT THAT WAY! HOME!
GUESS I SHOULD BE GLAD HE NEVER COMES HOME WITH ANY BONES. ≈SIGH.≈
YOU CAN COME OUT NOW. NO VAMPIRE, JUST TOGO CHASING SOME GUY WHO WAS PROBABLY ALLERGIC!
WE KNEW THAT!
YEAH, I WAS JUST SAYING THAT WHOLE THING ABOUT THE ALLERGY TO BESS.

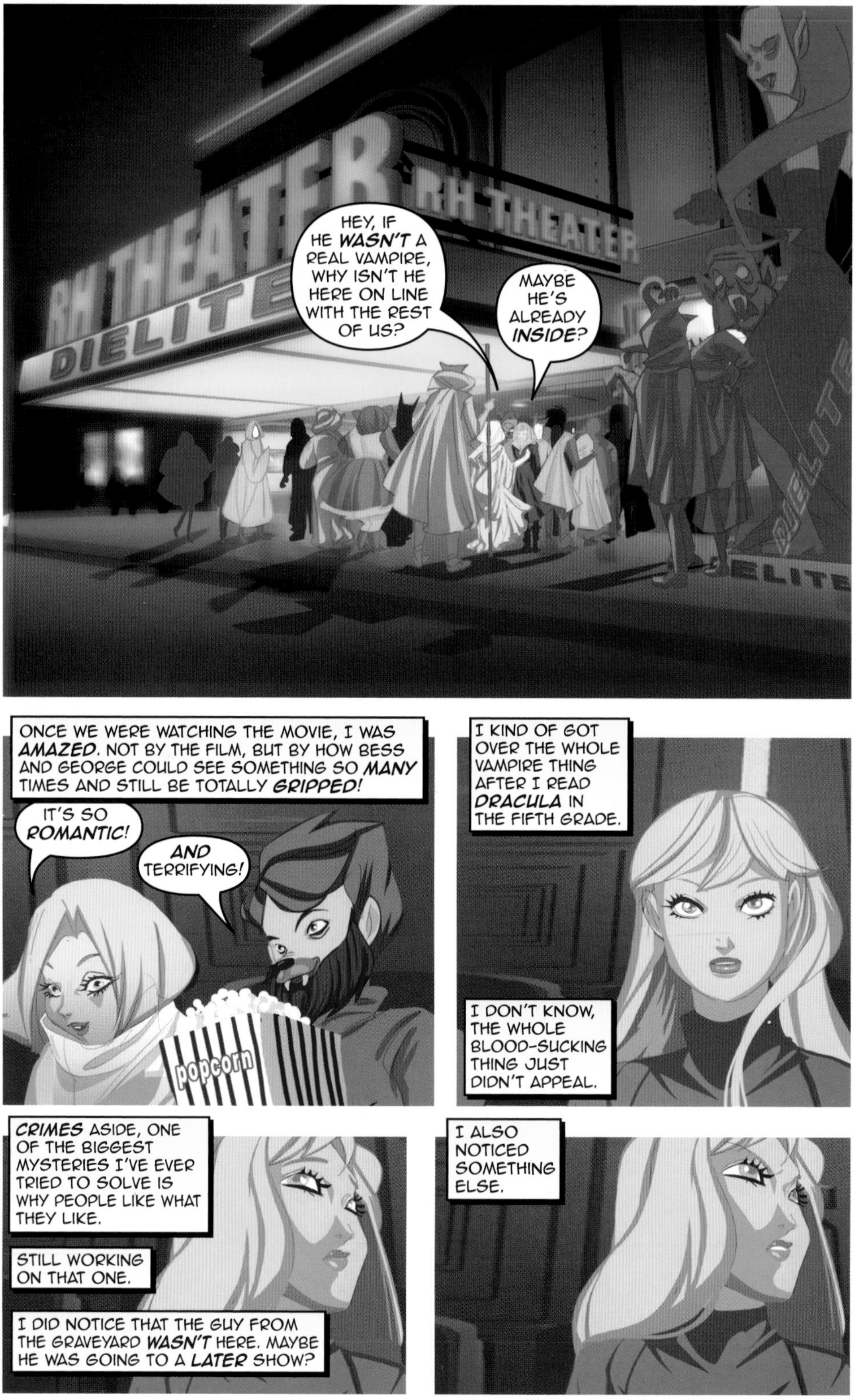

RH THEATER
DIELITE
HEY, IF HE WASN'T A REAL VAMPIRE, WHY ISN'T HE HERE ON LINE WITH THE REST OF US?
MAYBE HE'S ALREADY INSIDE?
ONCE WE WERE WATCHING THE MOVIE, I WAS AMAZED. NOT BY THE FILM, BUT BY HOW BESS AND GEORGE COULD SEE SOMETHING SO MANY TIMES AND STILL BE TOTALLY GRIPPED!
IT'S SO ROMANTIC!
AND TERRIFYING!
popcorn
I KIND OF GOT OVER THE WHOLE VAMPIRE THING AFTER I READ DRACULA IN THE FIFTH GRADE.
I DON'T KNOW, THE WHOLE BLOOD-SUCKING THING JUST DIDN'T APPEAL.
CRIMES ASIDE, ONE OF THE BIGGEST MYSTERIES I'VE EVER TRIED TO SOLVE IS WHY PEOPLE LIKE WHAT THEY LIKE.
STILL WORKING ON THAT ONE.
I DID NOTICE THAT THE GUY FROM THE GRAVEYARD WASN'T HERE. MAYBE HE WAS GOING TO A LATER SHOW?
I ALSO NOTICED SOMETHING ELSE.

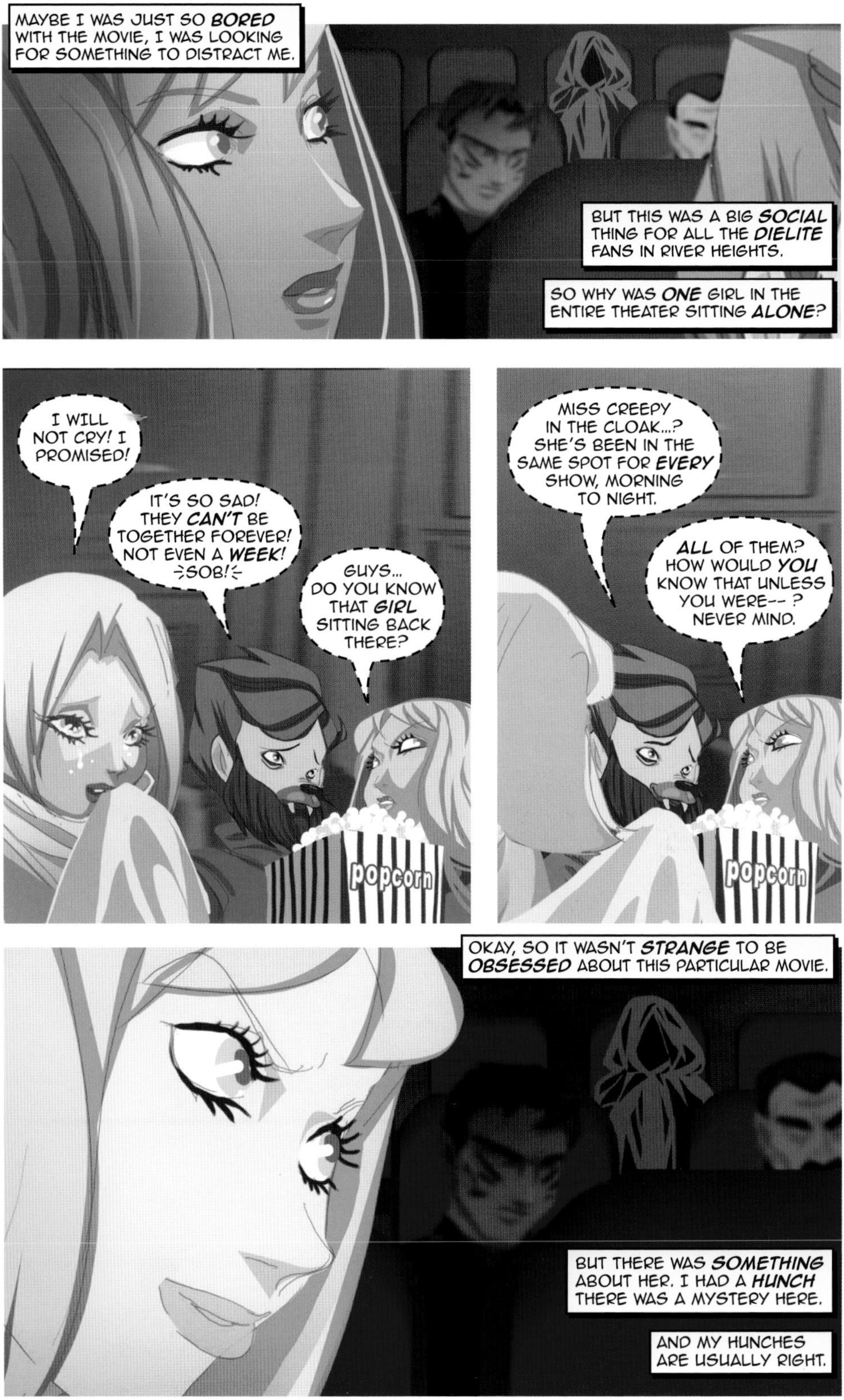
MAYBE I WAS JUST SO BORED WITH THE MOVIE, I WAS LOOKING FOR SOMETHING TO DISTRACT ME.
BUT THIS WAS A BIG SOCIAL THING FOR ALL THE DIELITE FANS IN RIVER HEIGHTS.
SO WHY WAS ONE GIRL IN THE ENTIRE THEATER SITTING ALONE?
I WILL NOT CRY! I PROMISED!
IT'S SO SAD! THEY CAN'T BE TOGETHER FOREVER! NOT EVEN A WEEK! SOB!
GUYS... DO YOU KNOW THAT GIRL SITTING BACK THERE?
popcorn
MISS CREEPY IN THE CLOAK...? SHE'S BEEN IN THE SAME SPOT FOR EVERY SHOW, MORNING TO NIGHT.
ALL OF THEM? HOW WOULD YOU KNOW THAT UNLESS YOU WERE-- ? NEVER MIND.
popcorn
OKAY, SO IT WASN'T STRANGE TO BE OBSESSED ABOUT THIS PARTICULAR MOVIE.
BUT THERE WAS SOMETHING ABOUT HER. I HAD A HUNCH THERE WAS A MYSTERY HERE.
AND MY HUNCHES ARE USUALLY RIGHT.

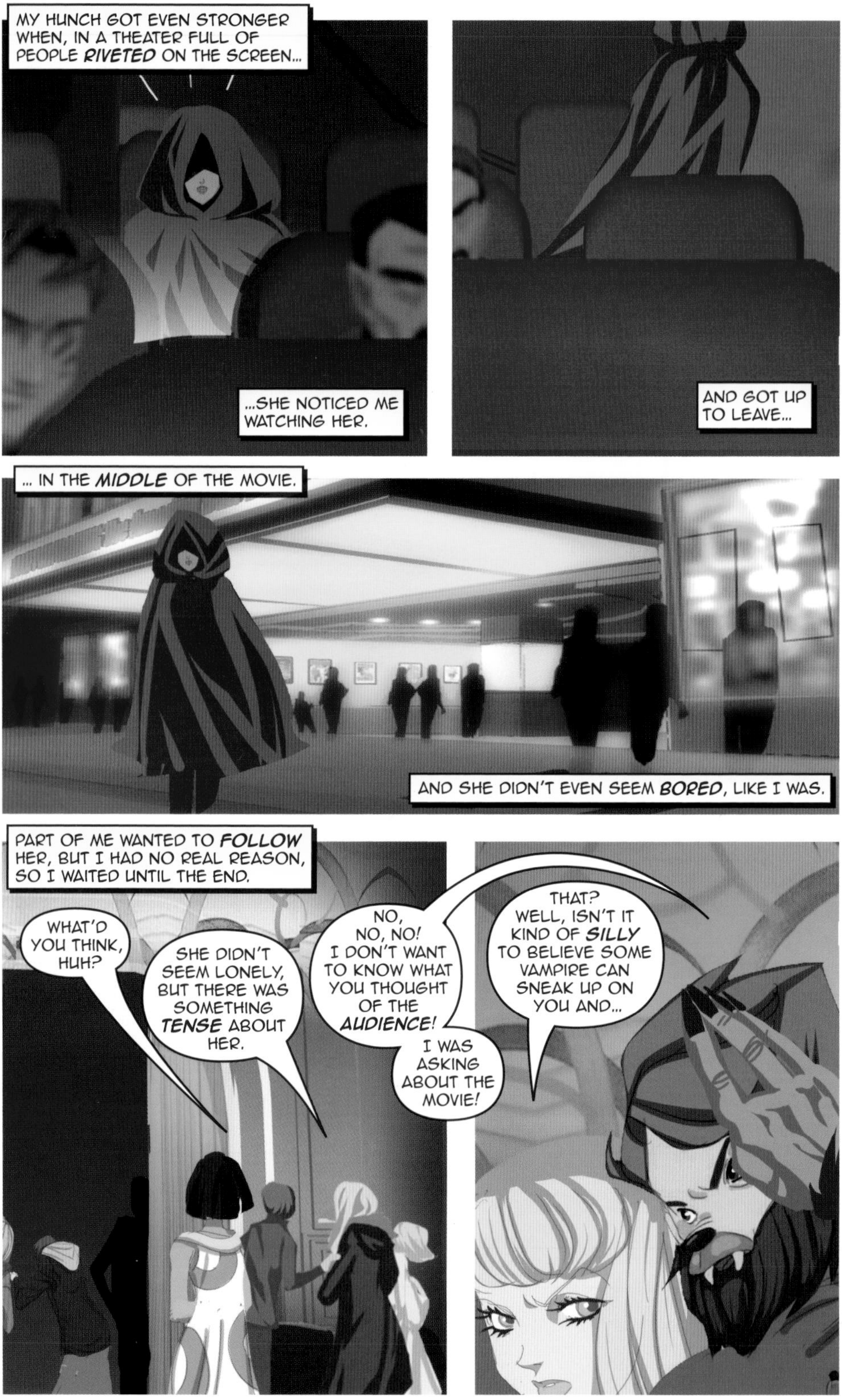
MY HUNCH GOT EVEN STRONGER WHEN, IN A THEATER FULL OF PEOPLE *RIVETED* ON THE SCREEN...
...SHE NOTICED ME WATCHING HER.
AND GOT UP TO LEAVE...
... IN THE *MIDDLE* OF THE MOVIE.
AND SHE DIDN'T EVEN SEEM *BORED*, LIKE I WAS.
PART OF ME WANTED TO *FOLLOW* HER, BUT I HAD NO REAL REASON, SO I WAITED UNTIL THE END.
WHAT'D YOU THINK, HUH?
SHE DIDN'T SEEM LONELY, BUT THERE WAS SOMETHING *TENSE* ABOUT HER.
NO, NO, NO! I DON'T WANT TO KNOW WHAT YOU THOUGHT OF THE *AUDIENCE*!
I WAS ASKING ABOUT THE MOVIE!
THAT? WELL, ISN'T IT KIND OF *SILLY* TO BELIEVE SOME VAMPIRE CAN SNEAK UP ON YOU AND...

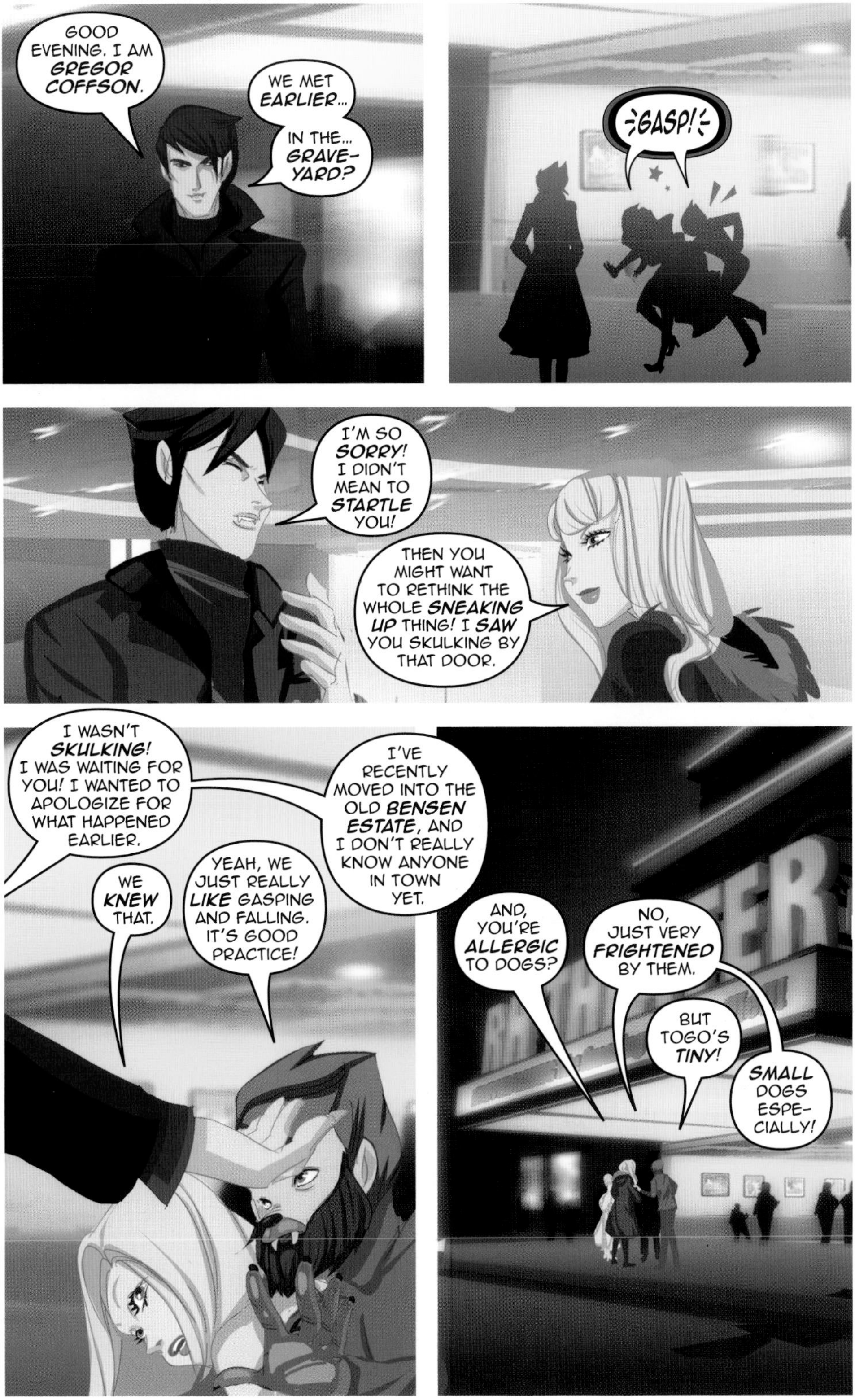
GOOD EVENING. I AM GREGOR COFFSON.
WE MET EARLIER...
IN THE... GRAVE-YARD?
GASP!
I'M SO SORRY! I DIDN'T MEAN TO STARTLE YOU!
THEN YOU MIGHT WANT TO RETHINK THE WHOLE SNEAKING UP THING! I SAW YOU SKULKING BY THAT DOOR.
I WASN'T SKULKING! I WAS WAITING FOR YOU! I WANTED TO APOLOGIZE FOR WHAT HAPPENED EARLIER.
I'VE RECENTLY MOVED INTO THE OLD BENSEN ESTATE, AND I DON'T REALLY KNOW ANYONE IN TOWN YET.
WE KNEW THAT.
YEAH, WE JUST REALLY LIKE GASPING AND FALLING. IT'S GOOD PRACTICE!
AND, YOU'RE ALLERGIC TO DOGS?
NO, JUST VERY FRIGHTENED BY THEM.
BUT TOGO'S TINY!
SMALL DOGS ESPE-CIALLY!

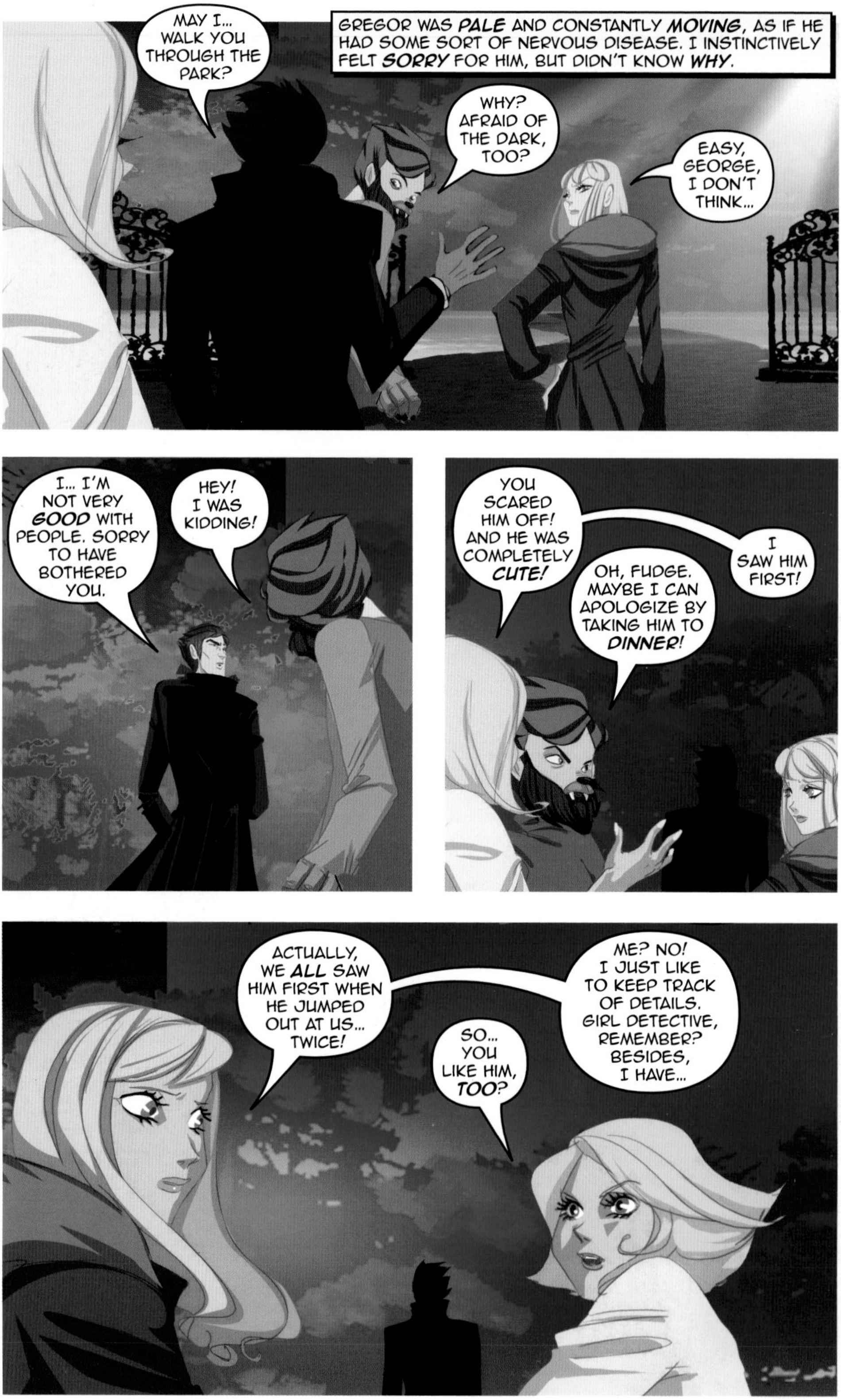
MAY I... WALK YOU THROUGH THE PARK?
GREGOR WAS PALE AND CONSTANTLY MOVING, AS IF HE HAD SOME SORT OF NERVOUS DISEASE. I INSTINCTIVELY FELT SORRY FOR HIM, BUT DIDN'T KNOW WHY.
WHY? AFRAID OF THE DARK, TOO?
EASY, GEORGE, I DON'T THINK...
I... I'M NOT VERY GOOD WITH PEOPLE. SORRY TO HAVE BOTHERED YOU.
HEY! I WAS KIDDING!
YOU SCARED HIM OFF! AND HE WAS COMPLETELY CUTE!
I SAW HIM FIRST!
OH, FUDGE. MAYBE I CAN APOLOGIZE BY TAKING HIM TO DINNER!
ACTUALLY, WE ALL SAW HIM FIRST WHEN HE JUMPED OUT AT US... TWICE!
ME? NO! I JUST LIKE TO KEEP TRACK OF DETAILS. GIRL DETECTIVE, REMEMBER? BESIDES, I HAVE...
SO... YOU LIKE HIM, TOO?

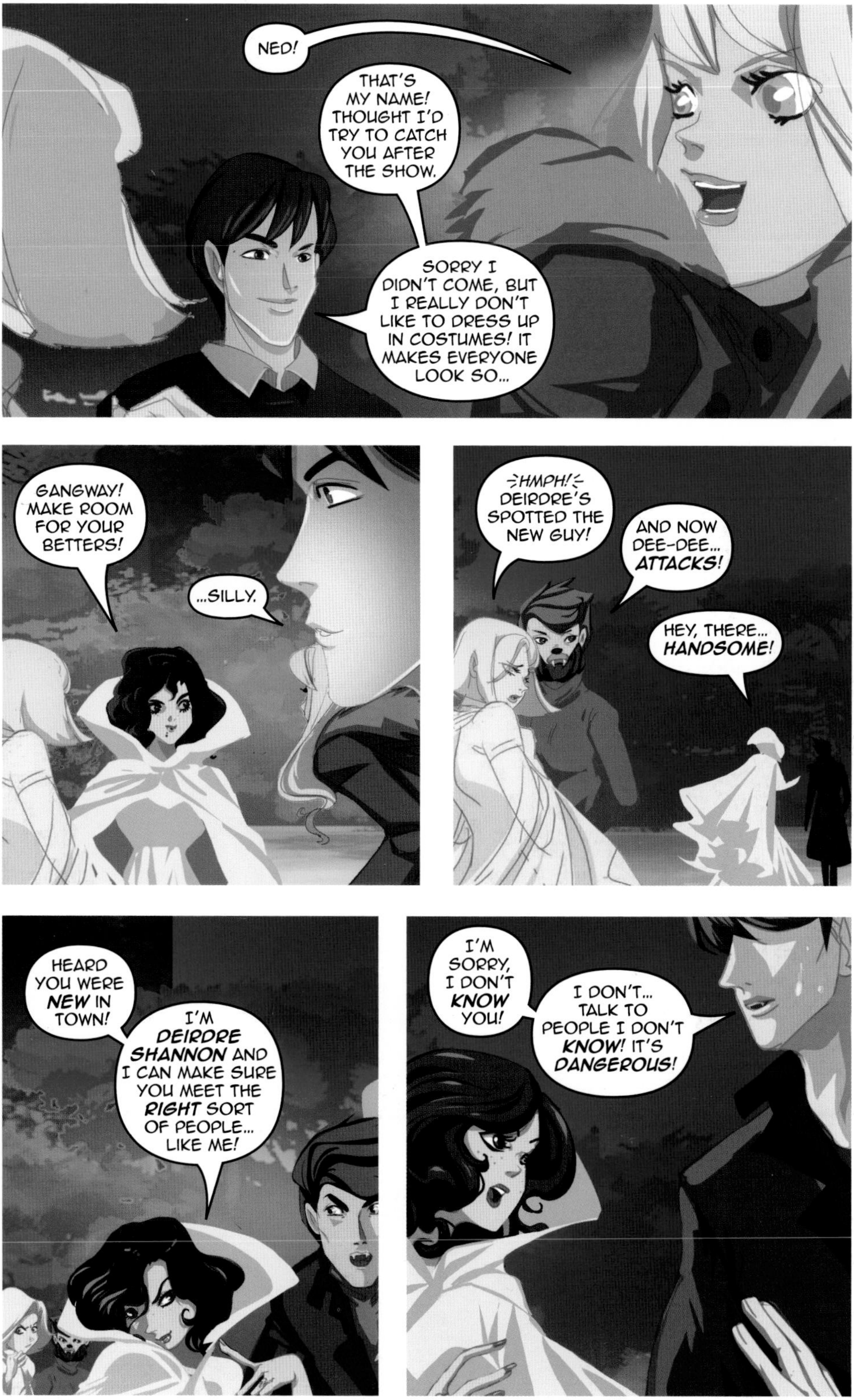
NED!
THAT'S MY NAME! THOUGHT I'D TRY TO CATCH YOU AFTER THE SHOW.
SORRY I DIDN'T COME, BUT I REALLY DON'T LIKE TO DRESS UP IN COSTUMES! IT MAKES EVERYONE LOOK SO...
GANGWAY! MAKE ROOM FOR YOUR BETTERS!
...SILLY.
HMPH! DEIRDRE'S SPOTTED THE NEW GUY!
AND NOW DEE-DEE... ATTACKS!
HEY, THERE... HANDSOME!
HEARD YOU WERE NEW IN TOWN!
I'M DEIRDRE SHANNON AND I CAN MAKE SURE YOU MEET THE RIGHT SORT OF PEOPLE... LIKE ME!
I'M SORRY, I DON'T KNOW YOU!
I DON'T... TALK TO PEOPLE I DON'T KNOW! IT'S DANGEROUS!

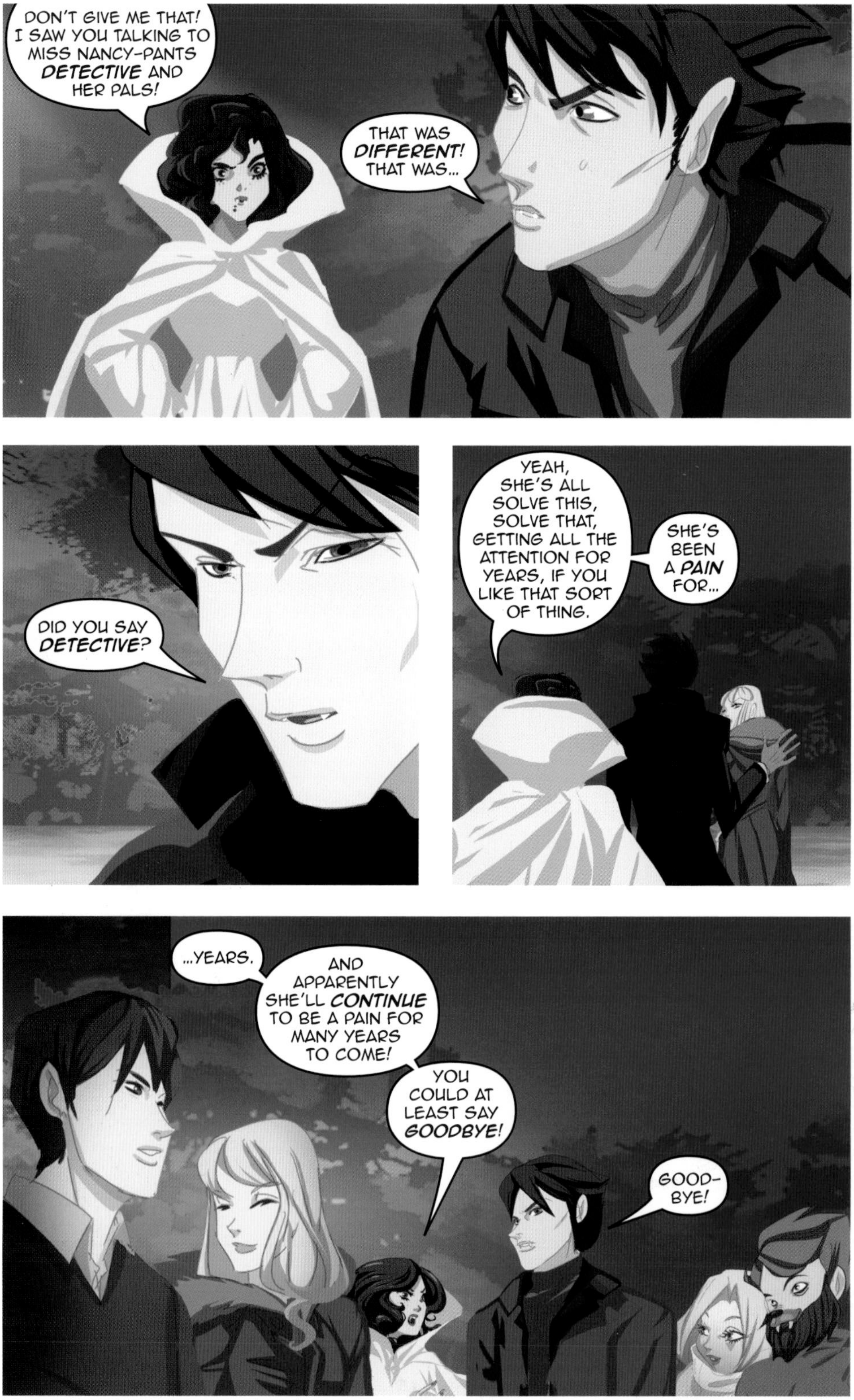
DON'T GIVE ME THAT! I SAW YOU TALKING TO MISS NANCY-PANTS DETECTIVE AND HER PALS!
THAT WAS DIFFERENT! THAT WAS...
DID YOU SAY DETECTIVE?
YEAH, SHE'S ALL SOLVE THIS, SOLVE THAT, GETTING ALL THE ATTENTION FOR YEARS, IF YOU LIKE THAT SORT OF THING.
SHE'S BEEN A PAIN FOR...
...YEARS.
AND APPARENTLY SHE'LL CONTINUE TO BE A PAIN FOR MANY YEARS TO COME!
YOU COULD AT LEAST SAY GOODBYE!
GOOD-BYE!

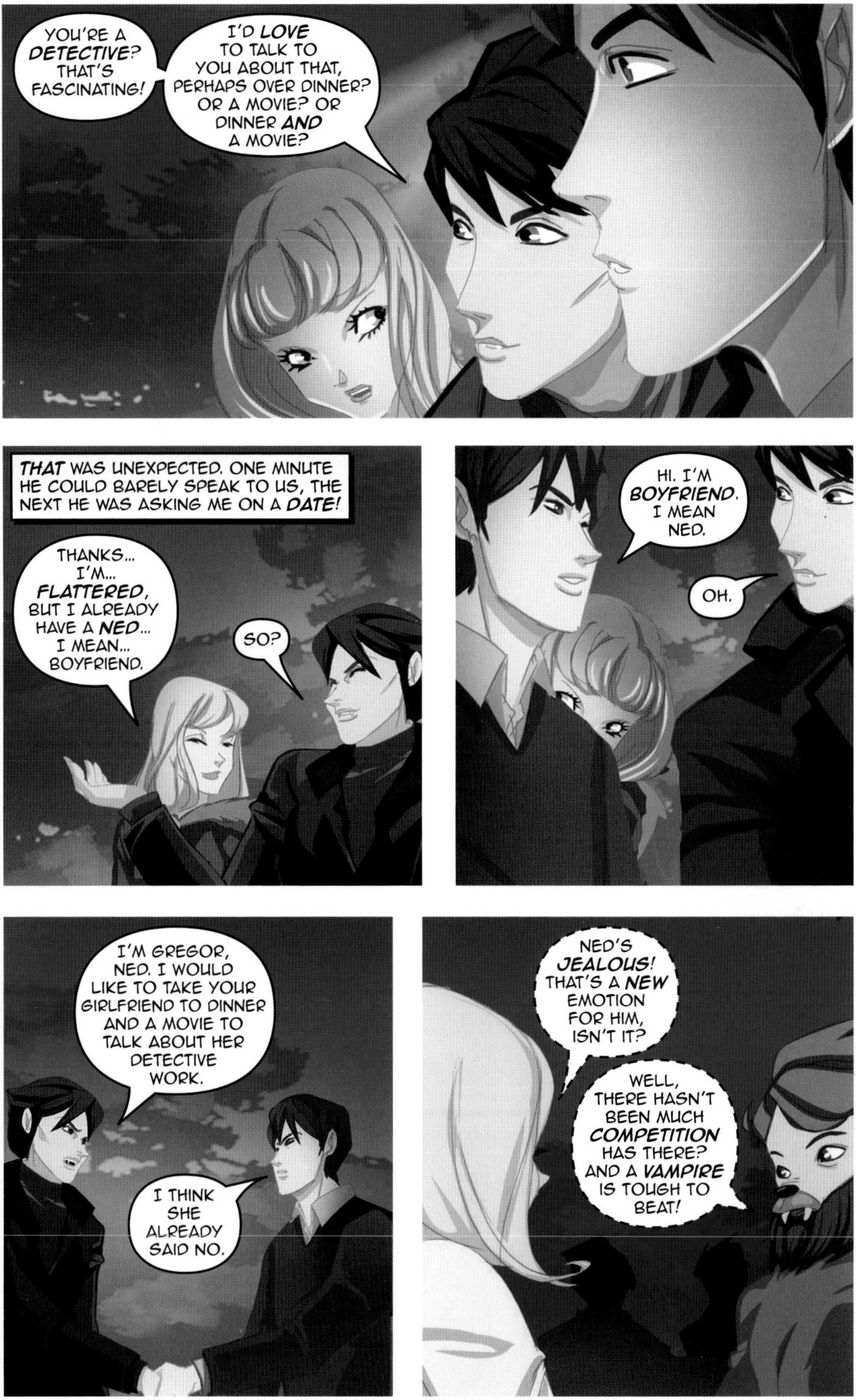
YOU'RE A DETECTIVE? THAT'S FASCINATING!
I'D LOVE TO TALK TO YOU ABOUT THAT, PERHAPS OVER DINNER? OR A MOVIE? OR DINNER AND A MOVIE?
THAT WAS UNEXPECTED. ONE MINUTE HE COULD BARELY SPEAK TO US, THE NEXT HE WAS ASKING ME ON A DATE!
THANKS... I'M... FLATTERED, BUT I ALREADY HAVE A NED... I MEAN... BOYFRIEND.
SO?
HI. I'M BOYFRIEND. I MEAN NED.
OH.
I'M GREGOR, NED. I WOULD LIKE TO TAKE YOUR GIRLFRIEND TO DINNER AND A MOVIE TO TALK ABOUT HER DETECTIVE WORK.
I THINK SHE ALREADY SAID NO.
NED'S JEALOUS! THAT'S A NEW EMOTION FOR HIM, ISN'T IT?
WELL, THERE HASN'T BEEN MUCH COMPETITION HAS THERE? AND A VAMPIRE IS TOUGH TO BEAT!

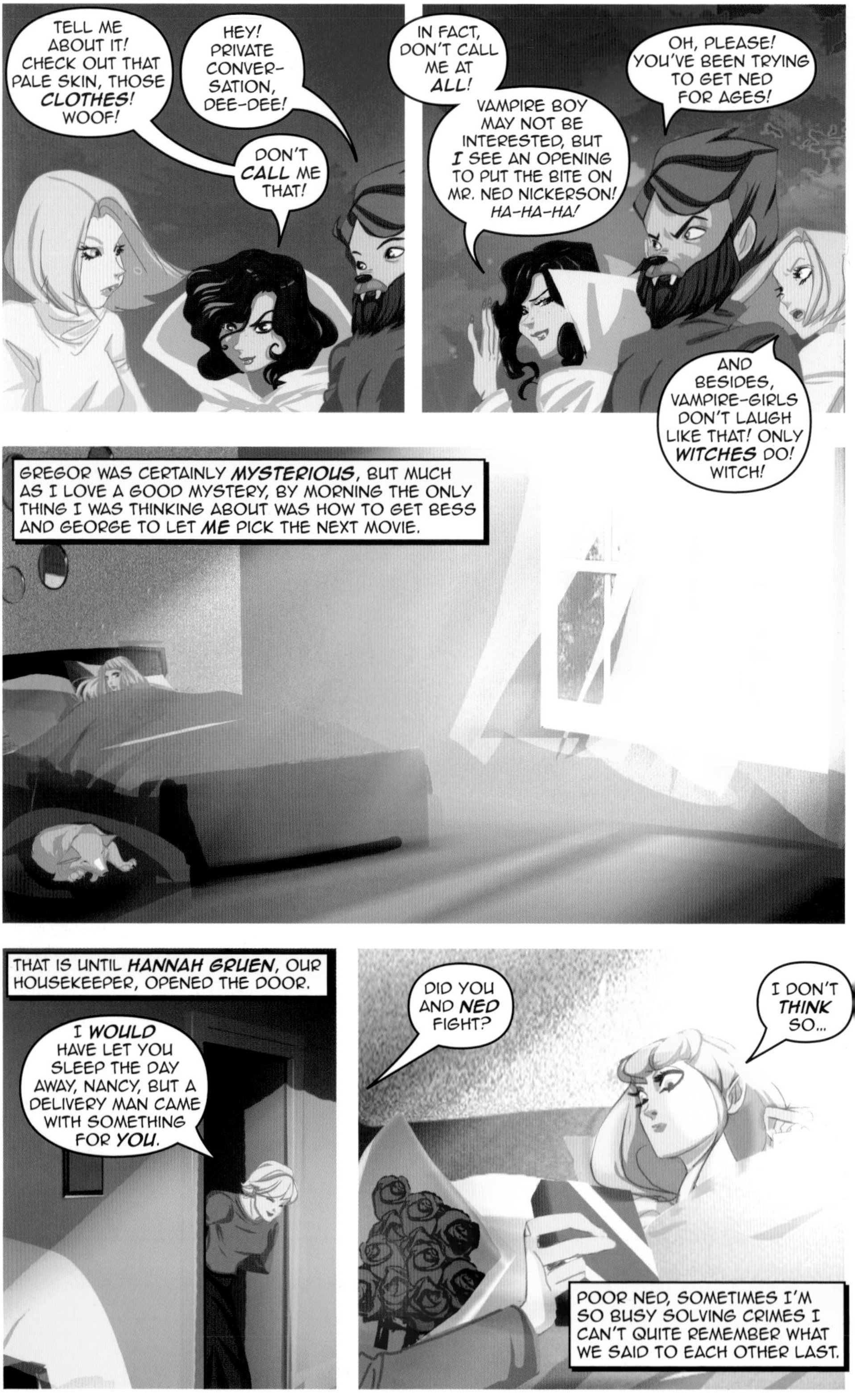

TELL ME ABOUT IT! CHECK OUT THAT PALE SKIN, THOSE CLOTHES! WOOF!
HEY! PRIVATE CONVER-SATION, DEE-DEE!
DON'T CALL ME THAT!
IN FACT, DON'T CALL ME AT ALL!
VAMPIRE BOY MAY NOT BE INTERESTED, BUT I SEE AN OPENING TO PUT THE BITE ON MR. NED NICKERSON! HA-HA-HA!
OH, PLEASE! YOU'VE BEEN TRYING TO GET NED FOR AGES!
AND BESIDES, VAMPIRE-GIRLS DON'T LAUGH LIKE THAT! ONLY WITCHES DO! WITCH!
GREGOR WAS CERTAINLY MYSTERIOUS, BUT MUCH AS I LOVE A GOOD MYSTERY, BY MORNING THE ONLY THING I WAS THINKING ABOUT WAS HOW TO GET BESS AND GEORGE TO LET ME PICK THE NEXT MOVIE.
THAT IS UNTIL HANNAH GRUEN, OUR HOUSEKEEPER, OPENED THE DOOR.
I WOULD HAVE LET YOU SLEEP THE DAY AWAY, NANCY, BUT A DELIVERY MAN CAME WITH SOMETHING FOR YOU.
DID YOU AND NED FIGHT?
I DON'T THINK SO...
POOR NED, SOMETIMES I'M SO BUSY SOLVING CRIMES I CAN'T QUITE REMEMBER WHAT WE SAID TO EACH OTHER LAST.

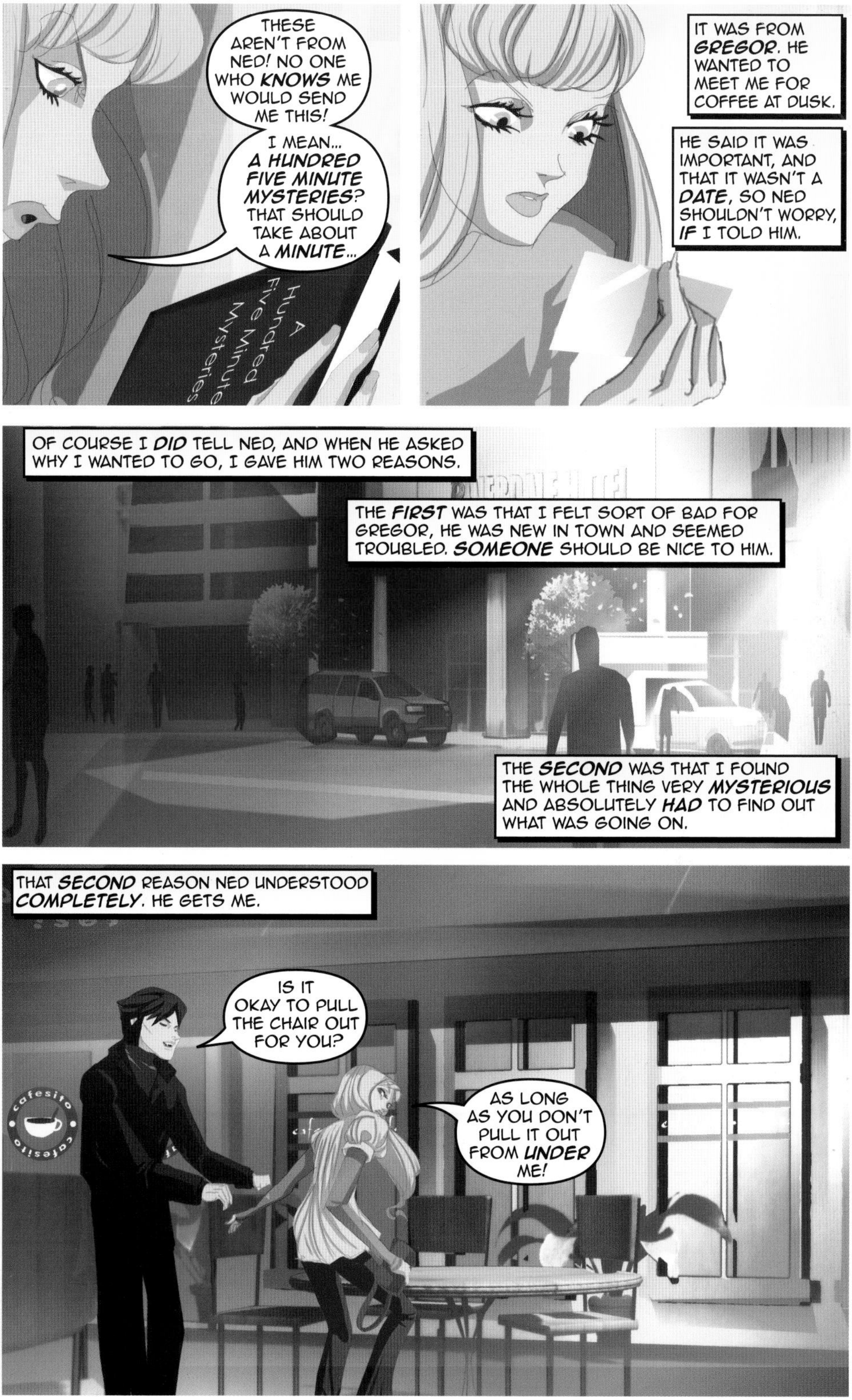

THESE AREN'T FROM NED! NO ONE WHO KNOWS ME WOULD SEND ME THIS!
I MEAN... A HUNDRED FIVE MINUTE MYSTERIES? THAT SHOULD TAKE ABOUT A MINUTE...
A Hundred Five Minute Mysteries
IT WAS FROM GREGOR. HE WANTED TO MEET ME FOR COFFEE AT DUSK.
HE SAID IT WAS IMPORTANT, AND THAT IT WASN'T A DATE, SO NED SHOULDN'T WORRY, IF I TOLD HIM.
OF COURSE I DID TELL NED, AND WHEN HE ASKED WHY I WANTED TO GO, I GAVE HIM TWO REASONS.
THE FIRST WAS THAT I FELT SORT OF BAD FOR GREGOR, HE WAS NEW IN TOWN AND SEEMED TROUBLED. SOMEONE SHOULD BE NICE TO HIM.
THE SECOND WAS THAT I FOUND THE WHOLE THING VERY MYSTERIOUS AND ABSOLUTELY HAD TO FIND OUT WHAT WAS GOING ON.
THAT SECOND REASON NED UNDERSTOOD COMPLETELY. HE GETS ME.
IS IT OKAY TO PULL THE CHAIR OUT FOR YOU?
cafesito
AS LONG AS YOU DON'T PULL IT OUT FROM UNDER ME!

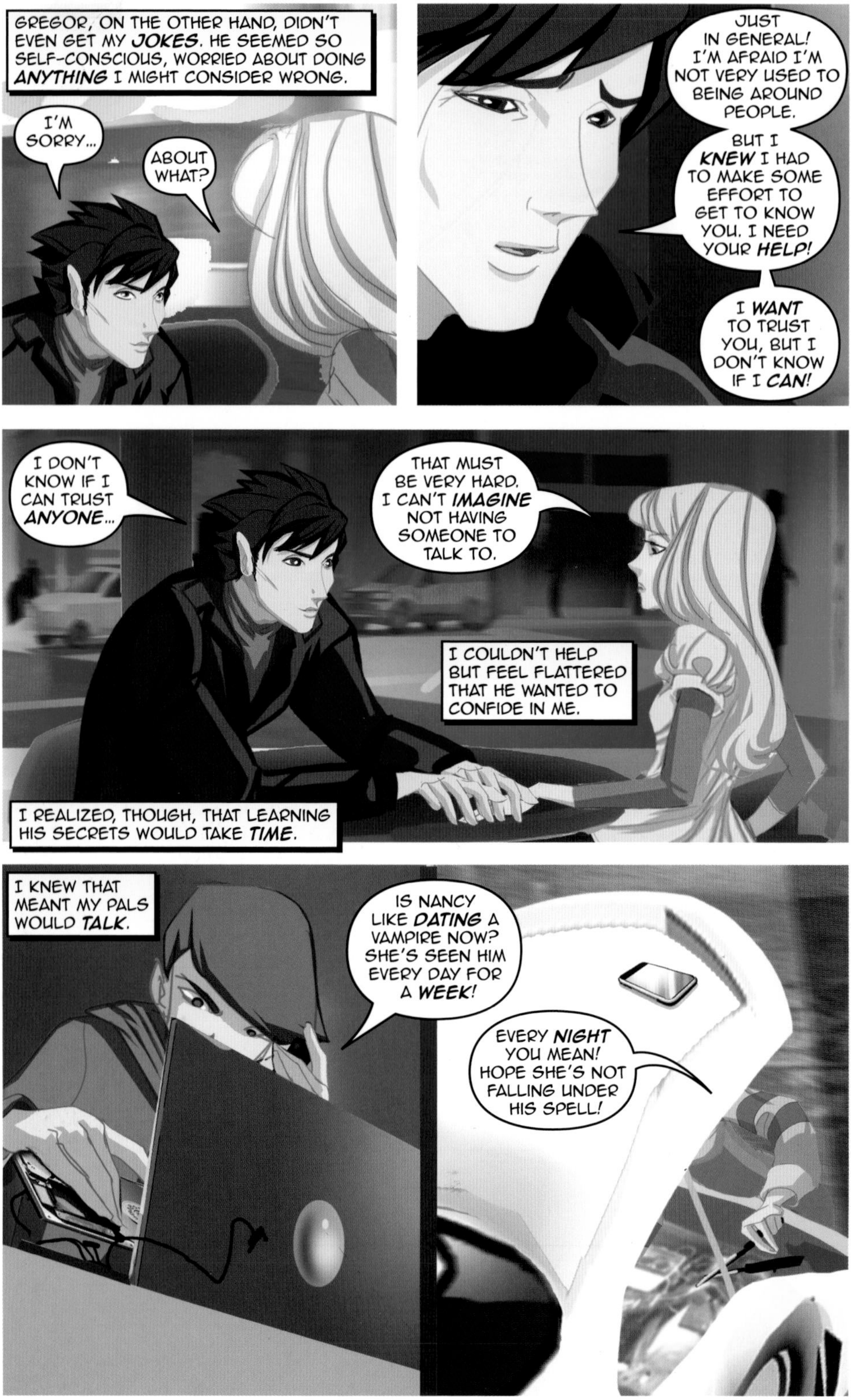
GREGOR, ON THE OTHER HAND, DIDN'T EVEN GET MY JOKES. HE SEEMED SO SELF-CONSCIOUS, WORRIED ABOUT DOING ANYTHING I MIGHT CONSIDER WRONG.
I'M SORRY...
ABOUT WHAT?
JUST IN GENERAL! I'M AFRAID I'M NOT VERY USED TO BEING AROUND PEOPLE.
BUT I KNEW I HAD TO MAKE SOME EFFORT TO GET TO KNOW YOU. I NEED YOUR HELP!
I WANT TO TRUST YOU, BUT I DON'T KNOW IF I CAN!
I DON'T KNOW IF I CAN TRUST ANYONE...
THAT MUST BE VERY HARD. I CAN'T IMAGINE NOT HAVING SOMEONE TO TALK TO.
I COULDN'T HELP BUT FEEL FLATTERED THAT HE WANTED TO CONFIDE IN ME.
I REALIZED, THOUGH, THAT LEARNING HIS SECRETS WOULD TAKE TIME.
I KNEW THAT MEANT MY PALS WOULD TALK.
IS NANCY LIKE DATING A VAMPIRE NOW? SHE'S SEEN HIM EVERY DAY FOR A WEEK!
EVERY NIGHT YOU MEAN! HOPE SHE'S NOT FALLING UNDER HIS SPELL!

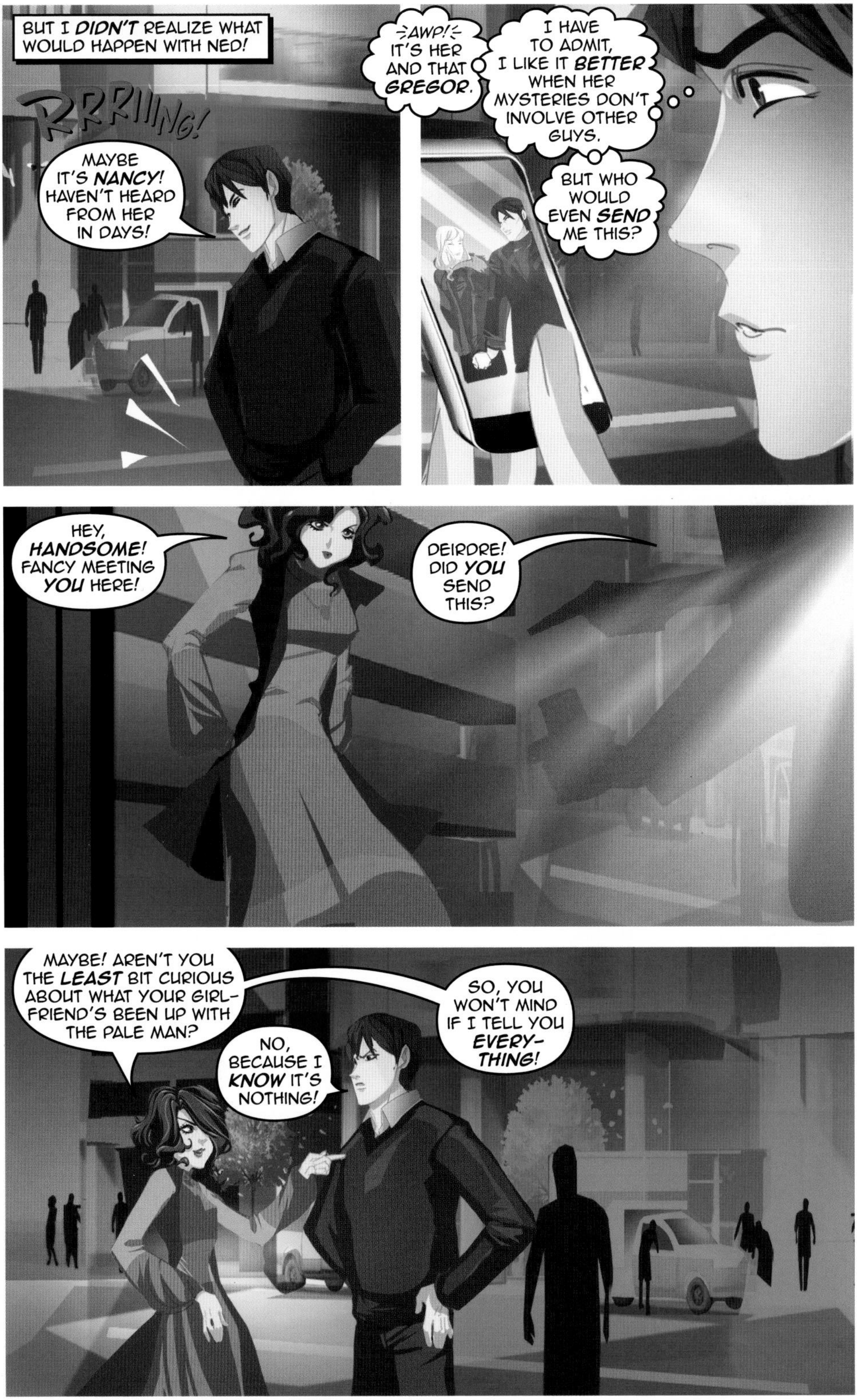
BUT I DIDN'T REALIZE WHAT WOULD HAPPEN WITH NED!
RRRIIING!
MAYBE IT'S NANCY! HAVEN'T HEARD FROM HER IN DAYS!
AWP! IT'S HER AND THAT GREGOR.
I HAVE TO ADMIT, I LIKE IT BETTER WHEN HER MYSTERIES DON'T INVOLVE OTHER GUYS.
BUT WHO WOULD EVEN SEND ME THIS?
HEY, HANDSOME! FANCY MEETING YOU HERE!
DEIRDRE! DID YOU SEND THIS?
MAYBE! AREN'T YOU THE LEAST BIT CURIOUS ABOUT WHAT YOUR GIRL-FRIEND'S BEEN UP WITH THE PALE MAN?
NO, BECAUSE I KNOW IT'S NOTHING!
SO, YOU WON'T MIND IF I TELL YOU EVERY-THING!

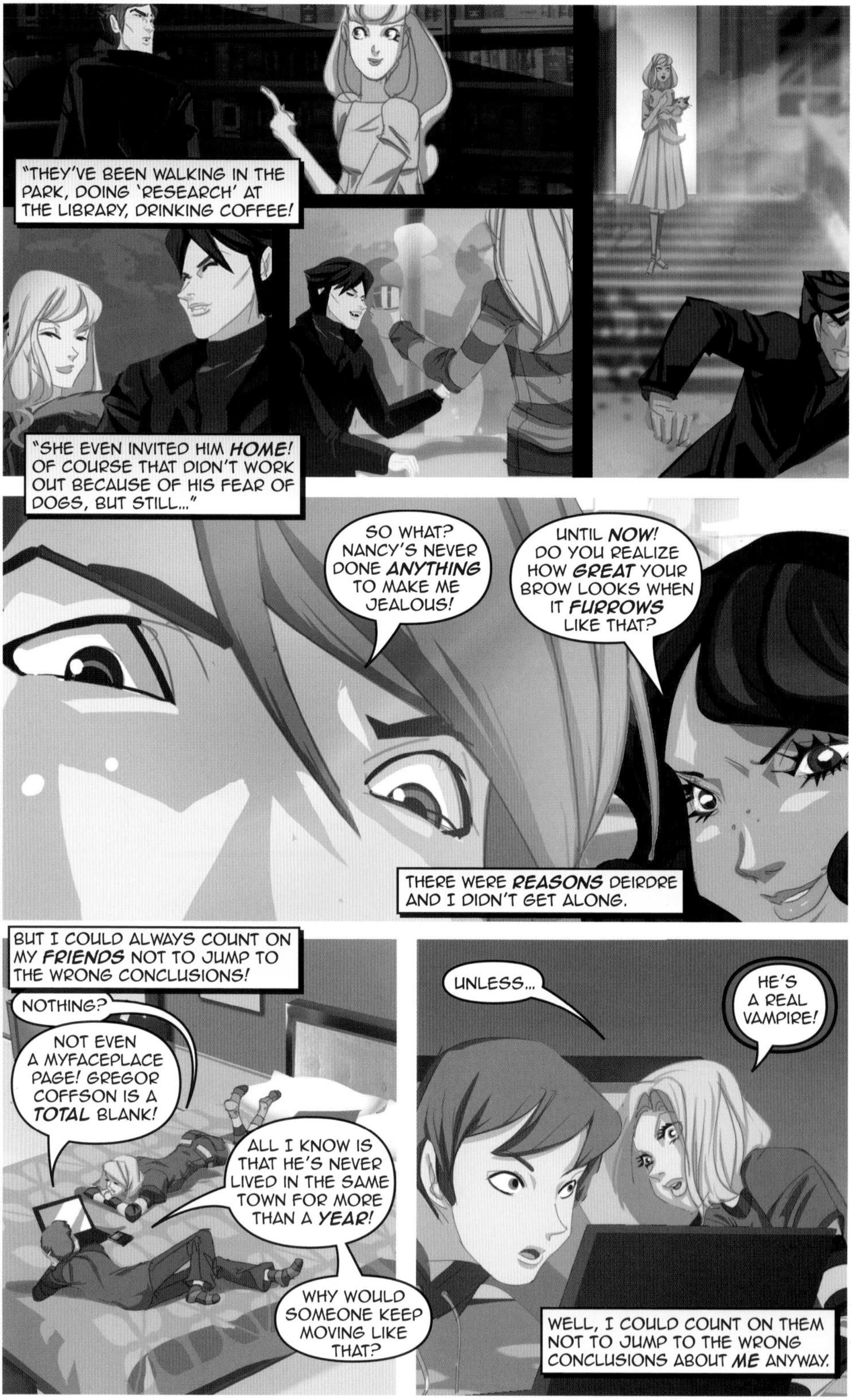
"THEY'VE BEEN WALKING IN THE PARK, DOING 'RESEARCH' AT THE LIBRARY, DRINKING COFFEE!
"SHE EVEN INVITED HIM *HOME*! OF COURSE THAT DIDN'T WORK OUT BECAUSE OF HIS FEAR OF DOGS, BUT STILL..."
SO WHAT? NANCY'S NEVER DONE *ANYTHING* TO MAKE ME JEALOUS!
UNTIL *NOW*! DO YOU REALIZE HOW *GREAT* YOUR BROW LOOKS WHEN IT *FURROWS* LIKE THAT?
THERE WERE *REASONS* DEIRDRE AND I DIDN'T GET ALONG.
BUT I COULD ALWAYS COUNT ON MY *FRIENDS* NOT TO JUMP TO THE WRONG CONCLUSIONS!
NOTHING?
NOT EVEN A MYFACEPLACE PAGE! GREGOR COFFSON IS A *TOTAL* BLANK!
ALL I KNOW IS THAT HE'S NEVER LIVED IN THE SAME TOWN FOR MORE THAN A *YEAR*!
WHY WOULD SOMEONE KEEP MOVING LIKE THAT?
UNLESS...
HE'S A REAL VAMPIRE!
WELL, I COULD COUNT ON THEM NOT TO JUMP TO THE WRONG CONCLUSIONS ABOUT *ME* ANYWAY.

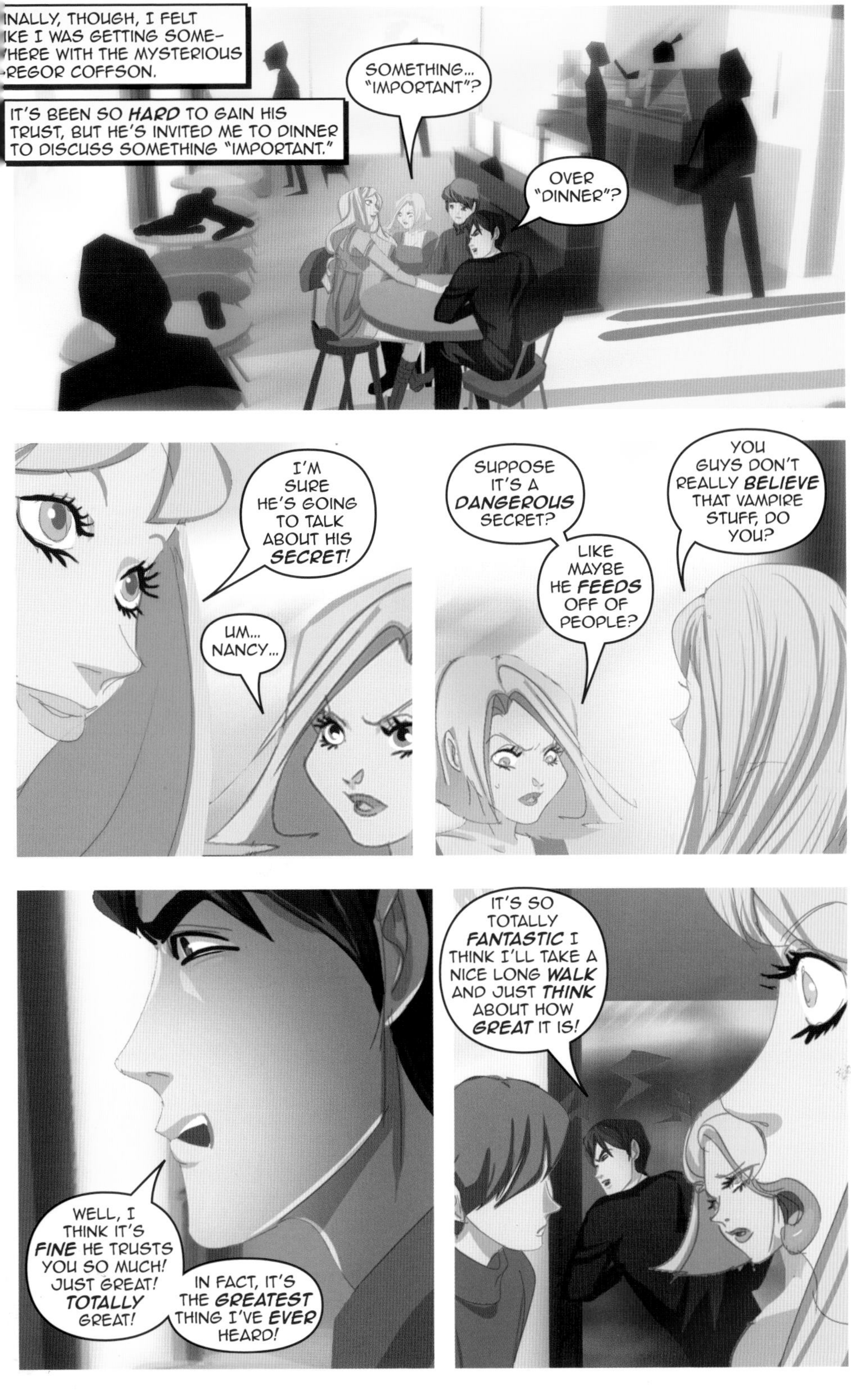
INALLY, THOUGH, I FELT IKE I WAS GETTING SOME- HERE WITH THE MYSTERIOUS REGOR COFFSON.
IT'S BEEN SO **HARD** TO GAIN HIS TRUST, BUT HE'S INVITED ME TO DINNER TO DISCUSS SOMETHING "IMPORTANT."
SOMETHING... "IMPORTANT"?
OVER "DINNER"?
I'M SURE HE'S GOING TO TALK ABOUT HIS **SECRET**!
UM... NANCY...
SUPPOSE IT'S A **DANGEROUS** SECRET?
LIKE MAYBE HE **FEEDS** OFF OF PEOPLE?
YOU GUYS DON'T REALLY **BELIEVE** THAT VAMPIRE STUFF, DO YOU?
WELL, I THINK IT'S **FINE** HE TRUSTS YOU SO MUCH! JUST GREAT! **TOTALLY** GREAT!
IN FACT, IT'S THE **GREATEST** THING I'VE **EVER** HEARD!
IT'S SO TOTALLY **FANTASTIC** I THINK I'LL TAKE A NICE LONG **WALK** AND JUST **THINK** ABOUT HOW **GREAT** IT IS!

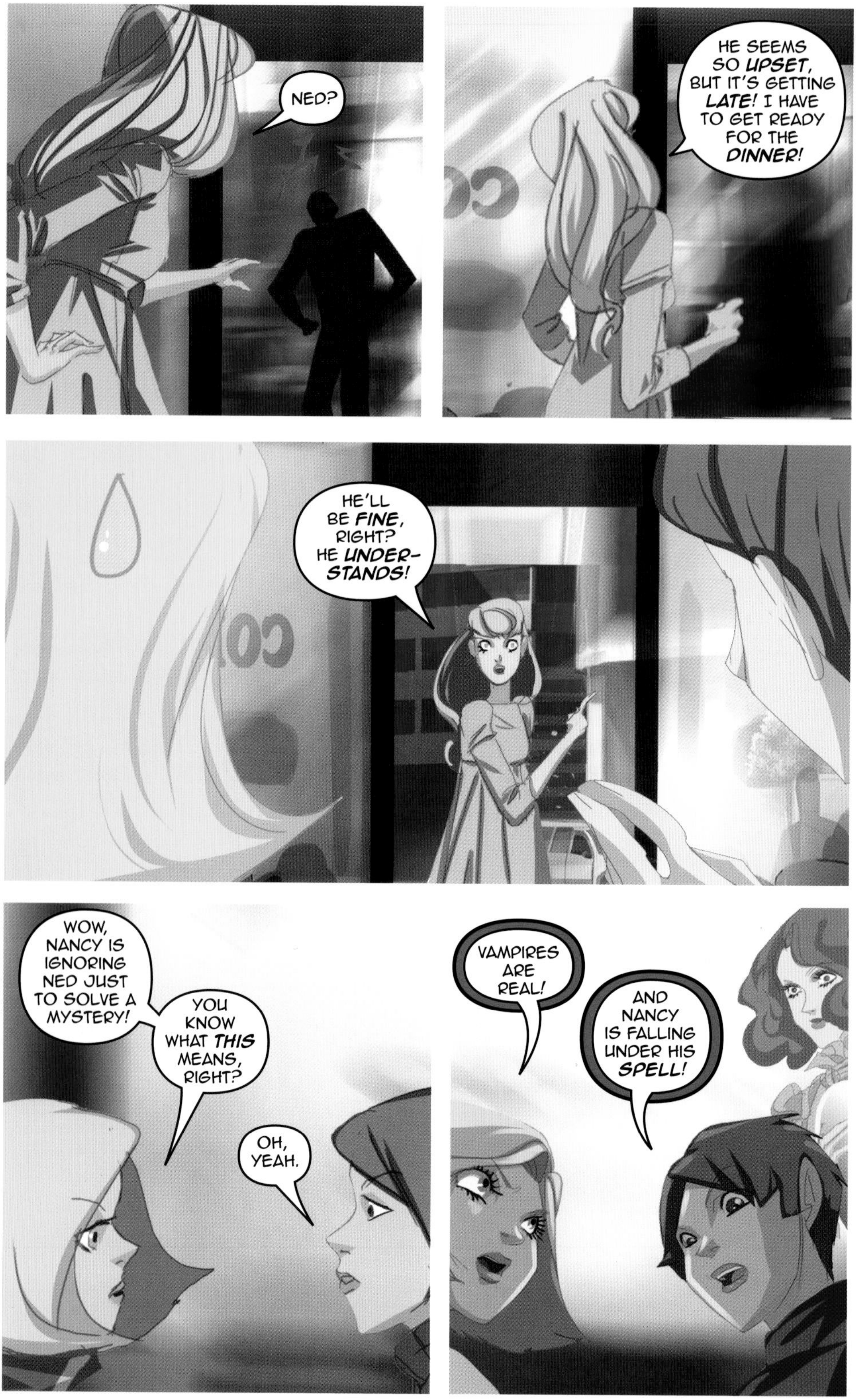
NED?
HE SEEMS SO UPSET, BUT IT'S GETTING LATE! I HAVE TO GET READY FOR THE DINNER!
HE'LL BE FINE, RIGHT? HE UNDER-STANDS!
WOW, NANCY IS IGNORING NED JUST TO SOLVE A MYSTERY!
YOU KNOW WHAT THIS MEANS, RIGHT?
OH, YEAH.
VAMPIRES ARE REAL!
AND NANCY IS FALLING UNDER HIS SPELL!

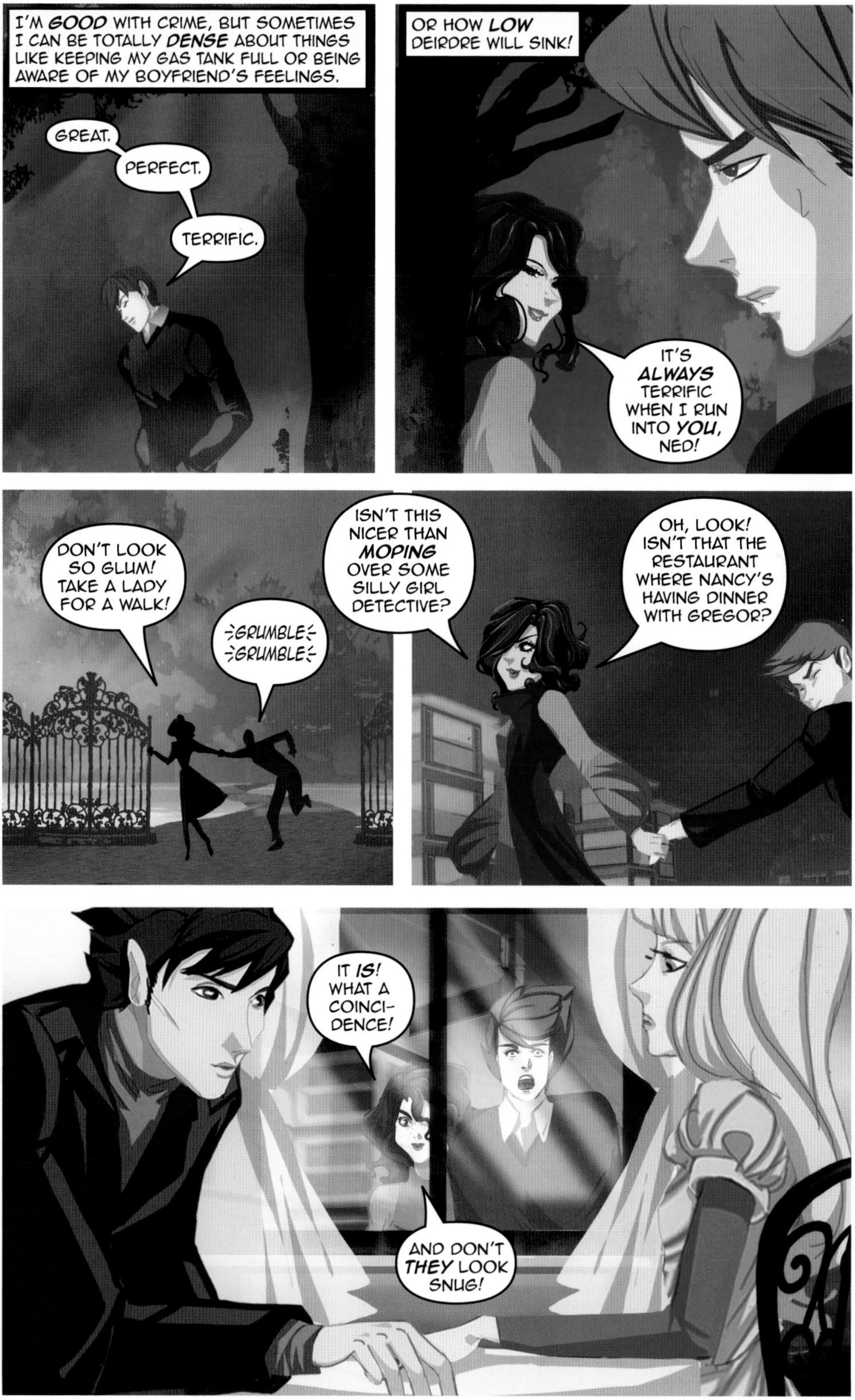
I'M GOOD WITH CRIME, BUT SOMETIMES I CAN BE TOTALLY DENSE ABOUT THINGS LIKE KEEPING MY GAS TANK FULL OR BEING AWARE OF MY BOYFRIEND'S FEELINGS.
GREAT.
PERFECT.
TERRIFIC.
OR HOW LOW DEIRDRE WILL SINK!
IT'S ALWAYS TERRIFIC WHEN I RUN INTO YOU, NED!
DON'T LOOK SO GLUM! TAKE A LADY FOR A WALK!
GRUMBLE GRUMBLE
ISN'T THIS NICER THAN MOPING OVER SOME SILLY GIRL DETECTIVE?
OH, LOOK! ISN'T THAT THE RESTAURANT WHERE NANCY'S HAVING DINNER WITH GREGOR?
IT IS! WHAT A COINCI-DENCE!
AND DON'T THEY LOOK SNUG!

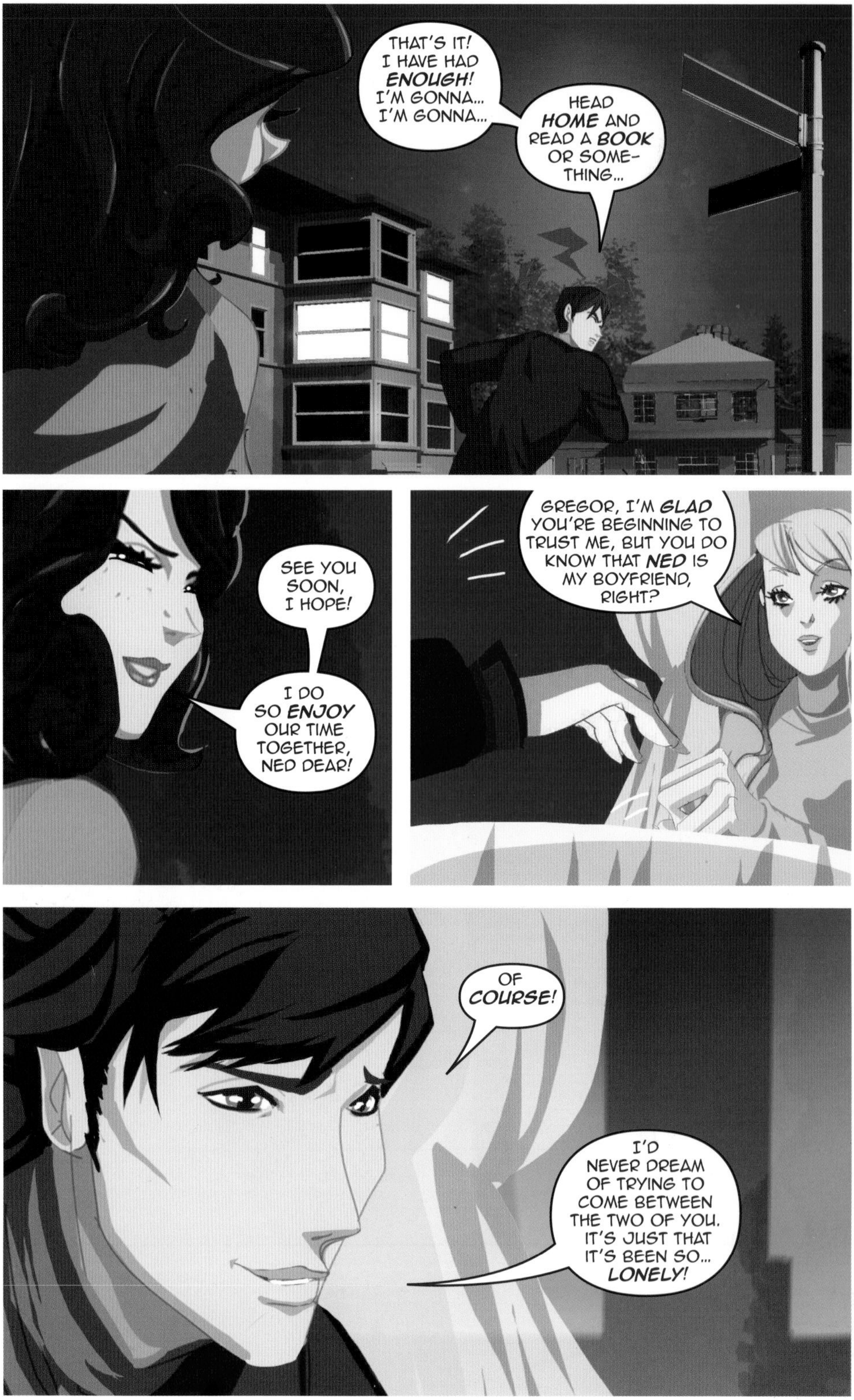
THAT'S IT! I HAVE HAD ENOUGH! I'M GONNA... I'M GONNA...
HEAD HOME AND READ A BOOK OR SOME-THING...
SEE YOU SOON, I HOPE!
I DO SO ENJOY OUR TIME TOGETHER, NED DEAR!
GREGOR, I'M GLAD YOU'RE BEGINNING TO TRUST ME, BUT YOU DO KNOW THAT NED IS MY BOYFRIEND, RIGHT?
OF COURSE!
I'D NEVER DREAM OF TRYING TO COME BETWEEN THE TWO OF YOU. IT'S JUST THAT IT'S BEEN SO... LONELY!

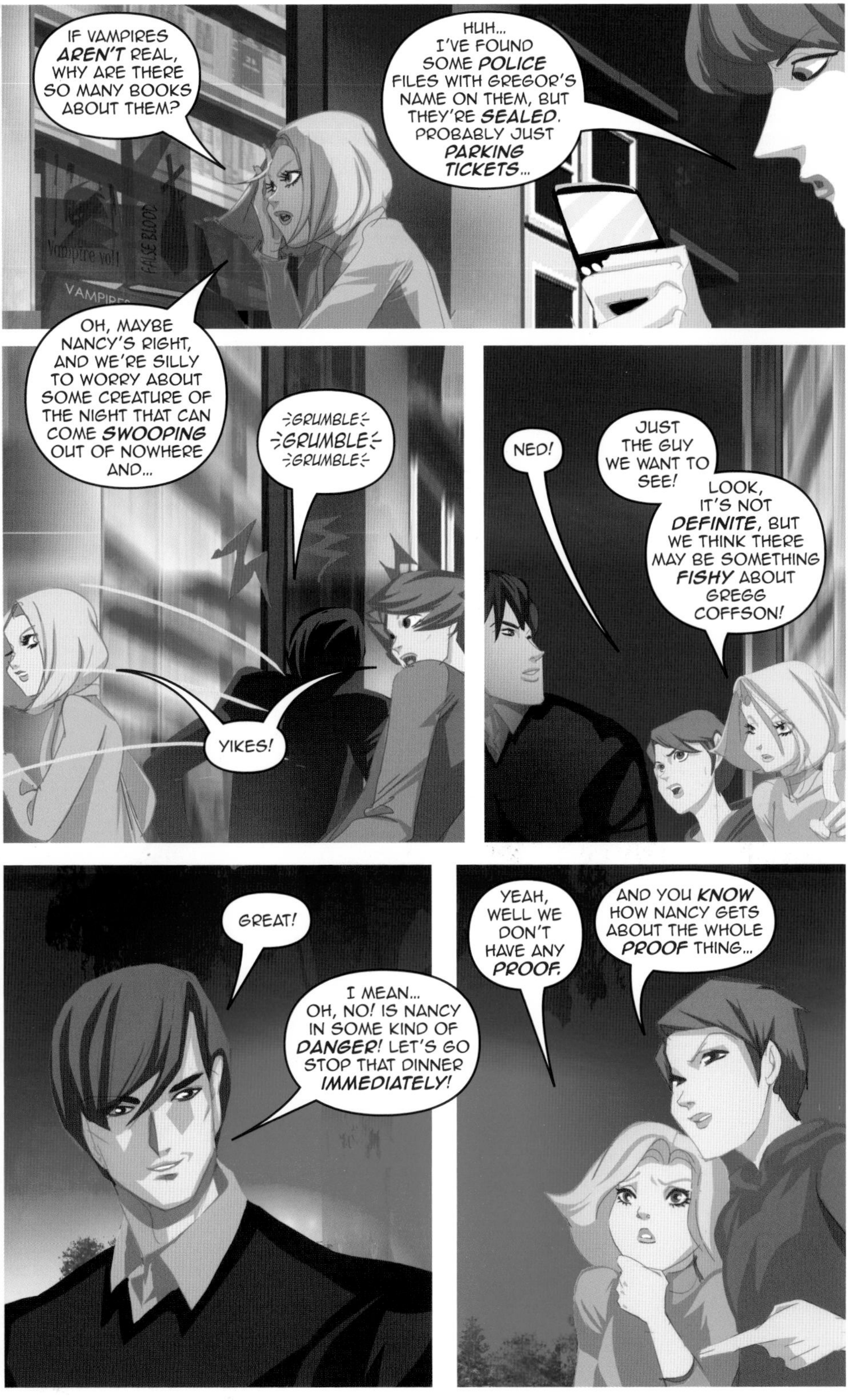

IF VAMPIRES AREN'T REAL, WHY ARE THERE SO MANY BOOKS ABOUT THEM?
HUH... I'VE FOUND SOME POLICE FILES WITH GREGOR'S NAME ON THEM, BUT THEY'RE SEALED. PROBABLY JUST PARKING TICKETS...
OH, MAYBE NANCY'S RIGHT, AND WE'RE SILLY TO WORRY ABOUT SOME CREATURE OF THE NIGHT THAT CAN COME SWOOPING OUT OF NOWHERE AND...
GRUMBLE GRUMBLE GRUMBLE
YIKES!
NED!
JUST THE GUY WE WANT TO SEE!
LOOK, IT'S NOT DEFINITE, BUT WE THINK THERE MAY BE SOMETHING FISHY ABOUT GREGG COFFSON!
GREAT!
I MEAN... OH, NO! IS NANCY IN SOME KIND OF DANGER! LET'S GO STOP THAT DINNER IMMEDIATELY!
YEAH, WELL WE DON'T HAVE ANY PROOF.
AND YOU KNOW HOW NANCY GETS ABOUT THE WHOLE PROOF THING...

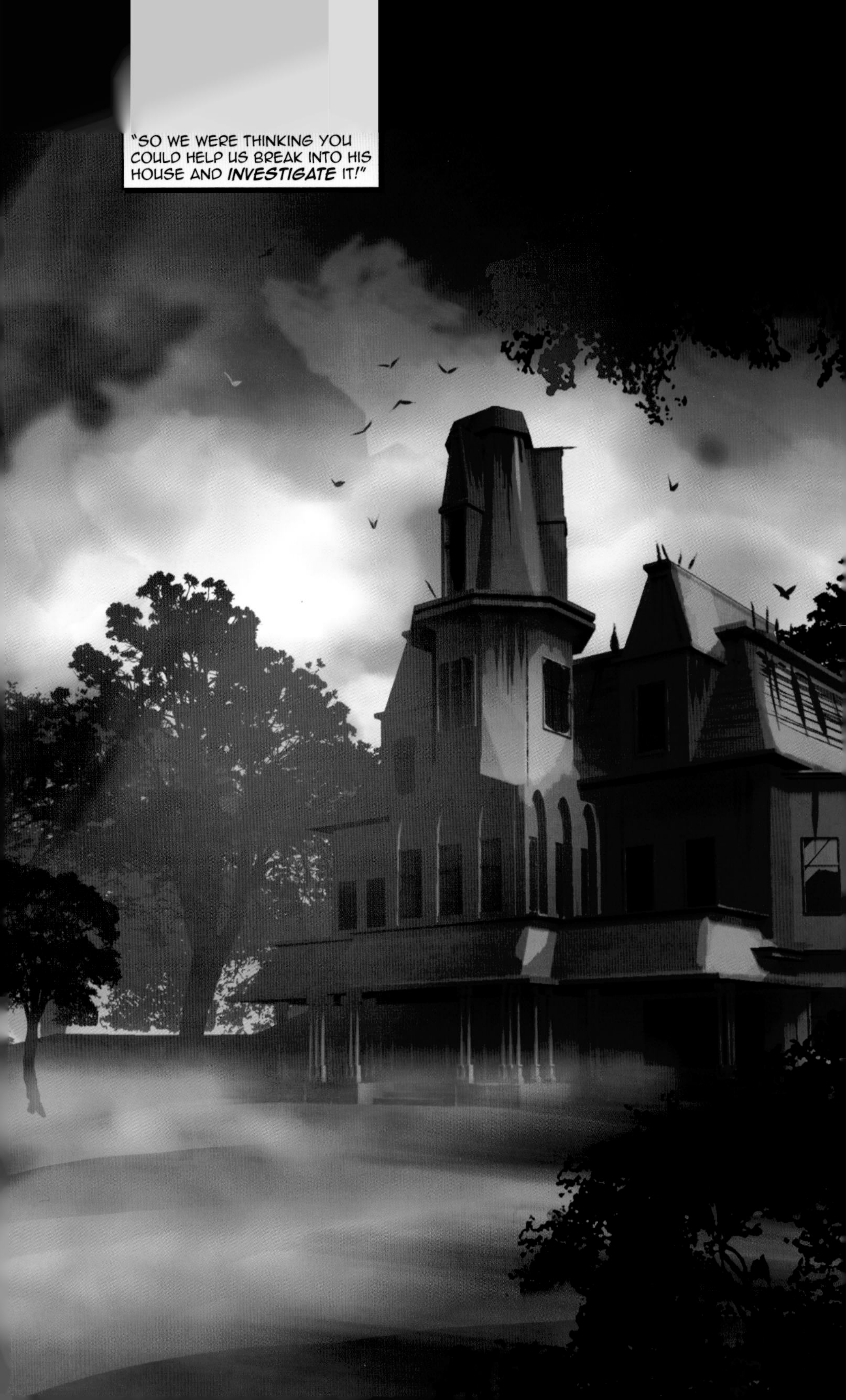
"SO WE WERE THINKING YOU COULD HELP US BREAK INTO HIS HOUSE AND INVESTIGATE IT!"

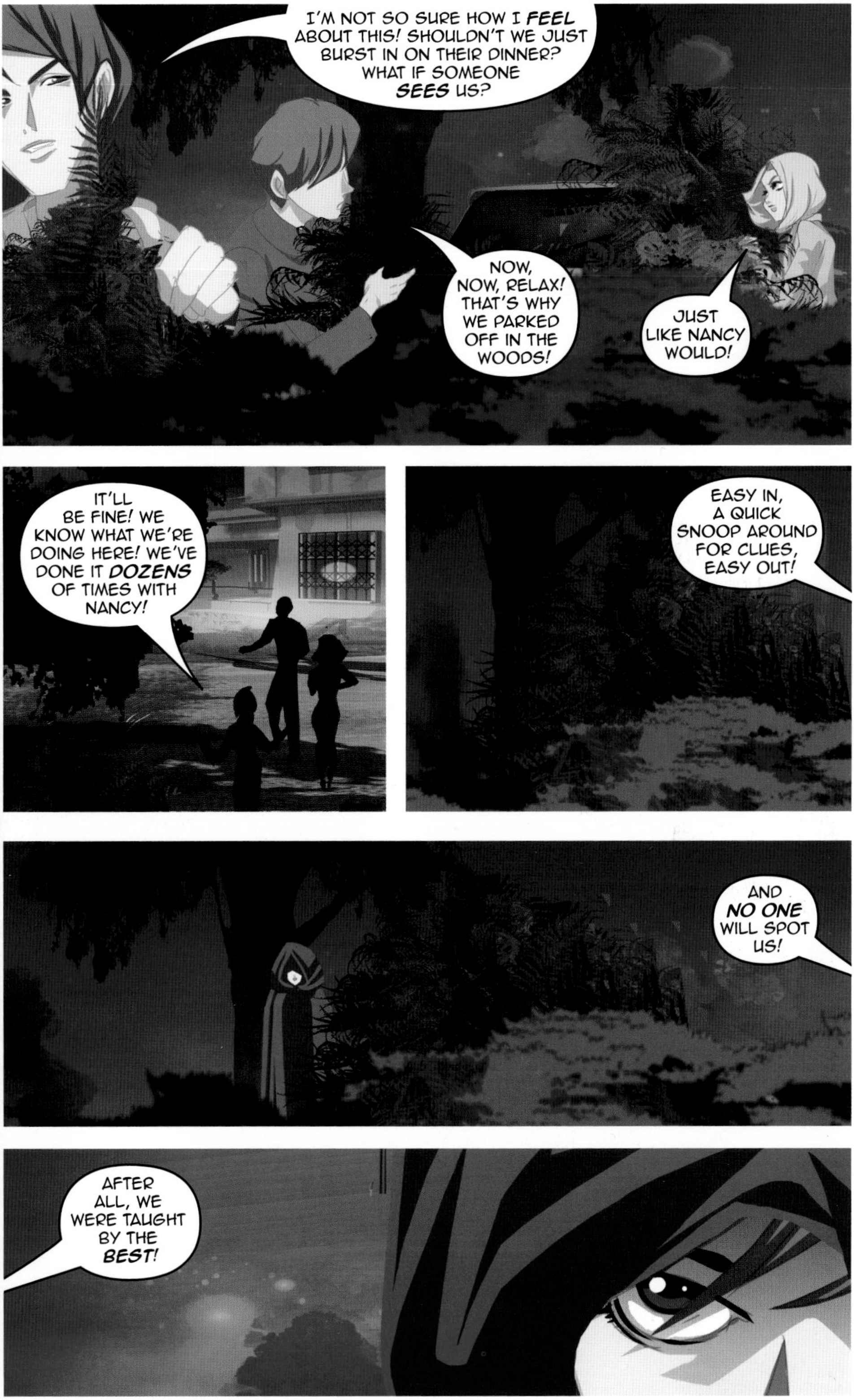
I'M NOT SO SURE HOW I *FEEL* ABOUT THIS! SHOULDN'T WE JUST BURST IN ON THEIR DINNER? WHAT IF SOMEONE *SEES* US?
NOW, NOW, RELAX! THAT'S WHY WE PARKED OFF IN THE WOODS!
JUST LIKE NANCY WOULD!
IT'LL BE FINE! WE KNOW WHAT WE'RE DOING HERE! WE'VE DONE IT *DOZENS* OF TIMES WITH NANCY!
EASY IN, A QUICK SNOOP AROUND FOR CLUES, EASY OUT!
AND *NO ONE* WILL SPOT US!
AFTER ALL, WE WERE TAUGHT BY THE *BEST*!

GET A LOAD OF THIS!
EVERY WINDOW'S COVERED BY THICK DRAPES!
THESE BABIES WOULDN'T LET A DROP OF SUNLIGHT IN.
BECAUSE MAYBE HE'S AFRAID SUNLIGHT WOULD DESTROY HIM?
OR MAYBE HE LIKES THE DARK!
I'M STARTING TO FEEL KIND OF SILLY ABOUT THIS.
DO YOU REALLY THINK THIS IS TIME FOR A SNACK?
NO, SILLY! BUT A VAMPIRE DOESN'T EAT THE WAY A NORMAL PERSON DOES.
IT SHOULD BE EMPTY, RIGHT?
OR NOT!
YIKES AND GASP!
THAT CAN'T BE WHAT IT LOOKS LIKE, CAN IT?
B-B-B-B-B-B-B-B-B-BLOOD?

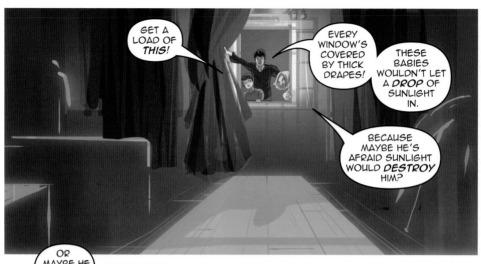

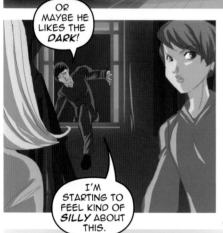

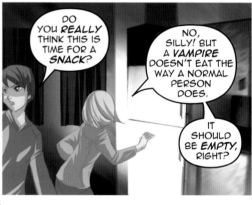

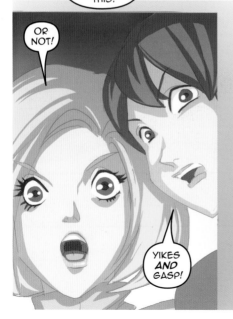

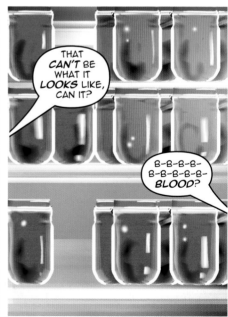

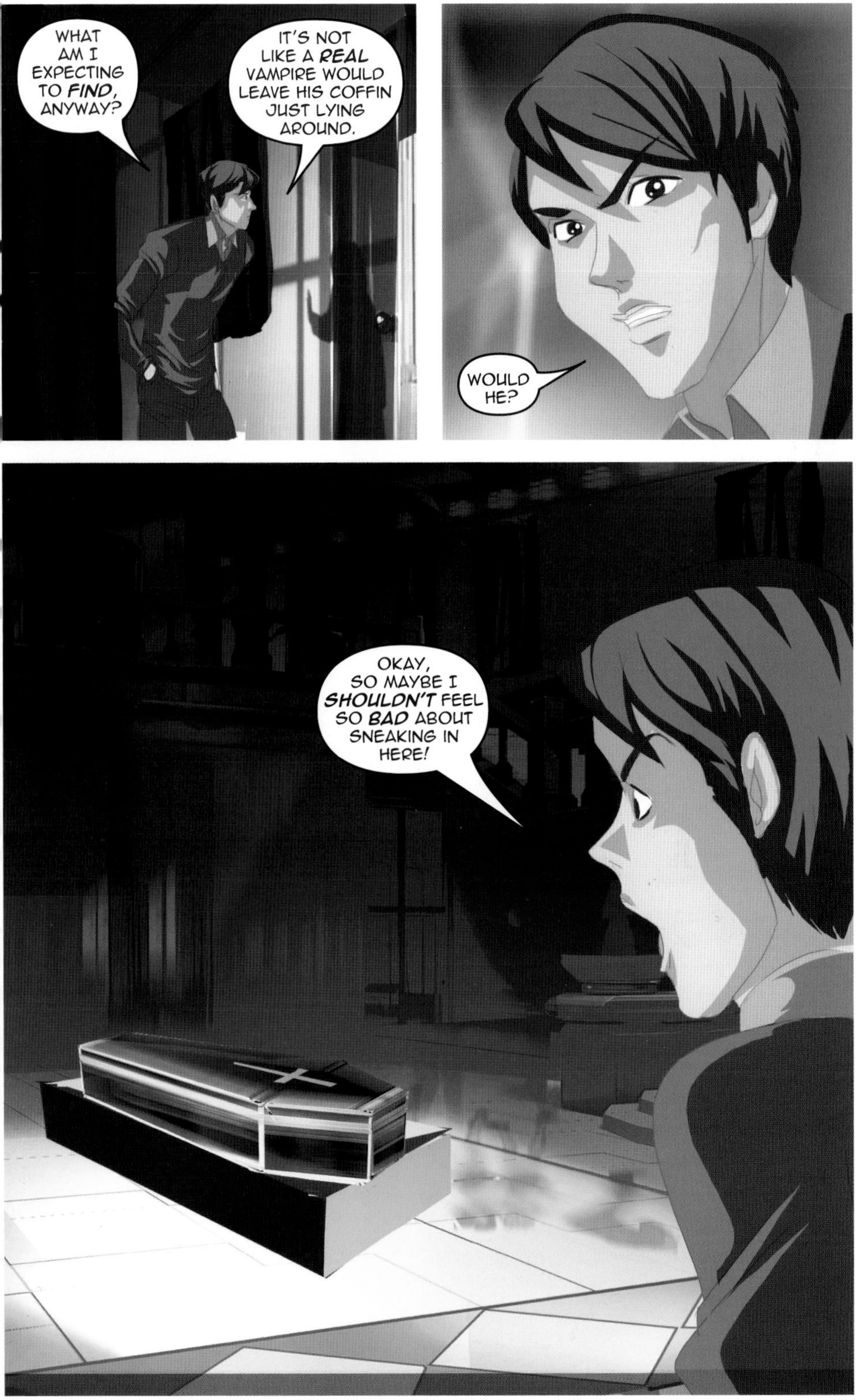
WHAT AM I EXPECTING TO FIND, ANYWAY?
IT'S NOT LIKE A REAL VAMPIRE WOULD LEAVE HIS COFFIN JUST LYING AROUND.
WOULD HE?
OKAY, SO MAYBE I SHOULDN'T FEEL SO BAD ABOUT SNEAKING IN HERE!

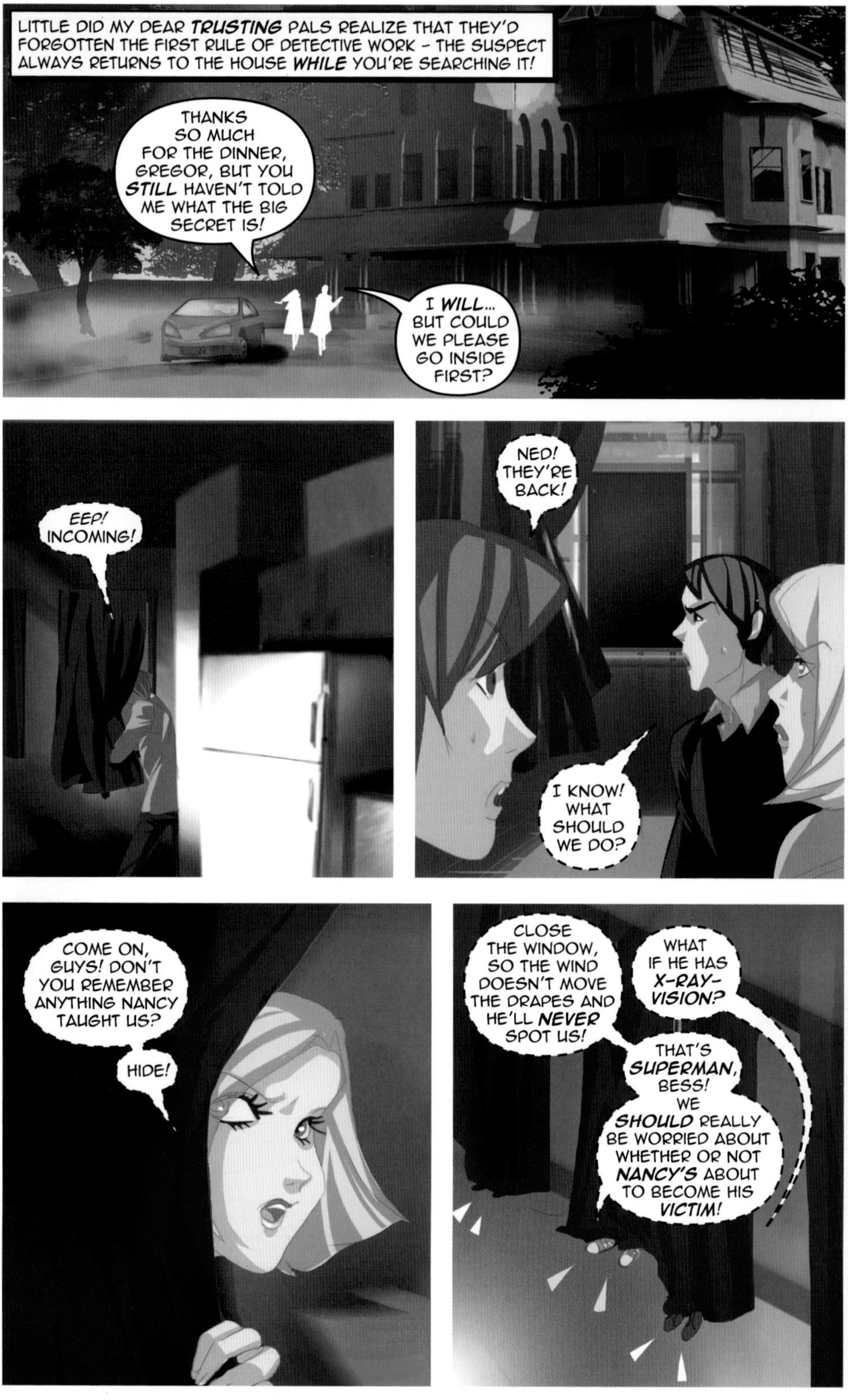
LITTLE DID MY DEAR TRUSTING PALS REALIZE THAT THEY'D FORGOTTEN THE FIRST RULE OF DETECTIVE WORK – THE SUSPECT ALWAYS RETURNS TO THE HOUSE WHILE YOU'RE SEARCHING IT!
THANKS SO MUCH FOR THE DINNER, GREGOR, BUT YOU STILL HAVEN'T TOLD ME WHAT THE BIG SECRET IS!
I WILL... BUT COULD WE PLEASE GO INSIDE FIRST?
EEP! INCOMING!
NED! THEY'RE BACK!
I KNOW! WHAT SHOULD WE DO?
COME ON, GUYS! DON'T YOU REMEMBER ANYTHING NANCY TAUGHT US?
HIDE!
CLOSE THE WINDOW, SO THE WIND DOESN'T MOVE THE DRAPES AND HE'LL NEVER SPOT US!
WHAT IF HE HAS X-RAY-VISION?
THAT'S SUPERMAN, BESS! WE SHOULD REALLY BE WORRIED ABOUT WHETHER OR NOT NANCY'S ABOUT TO BECOME HIS VICTIM!

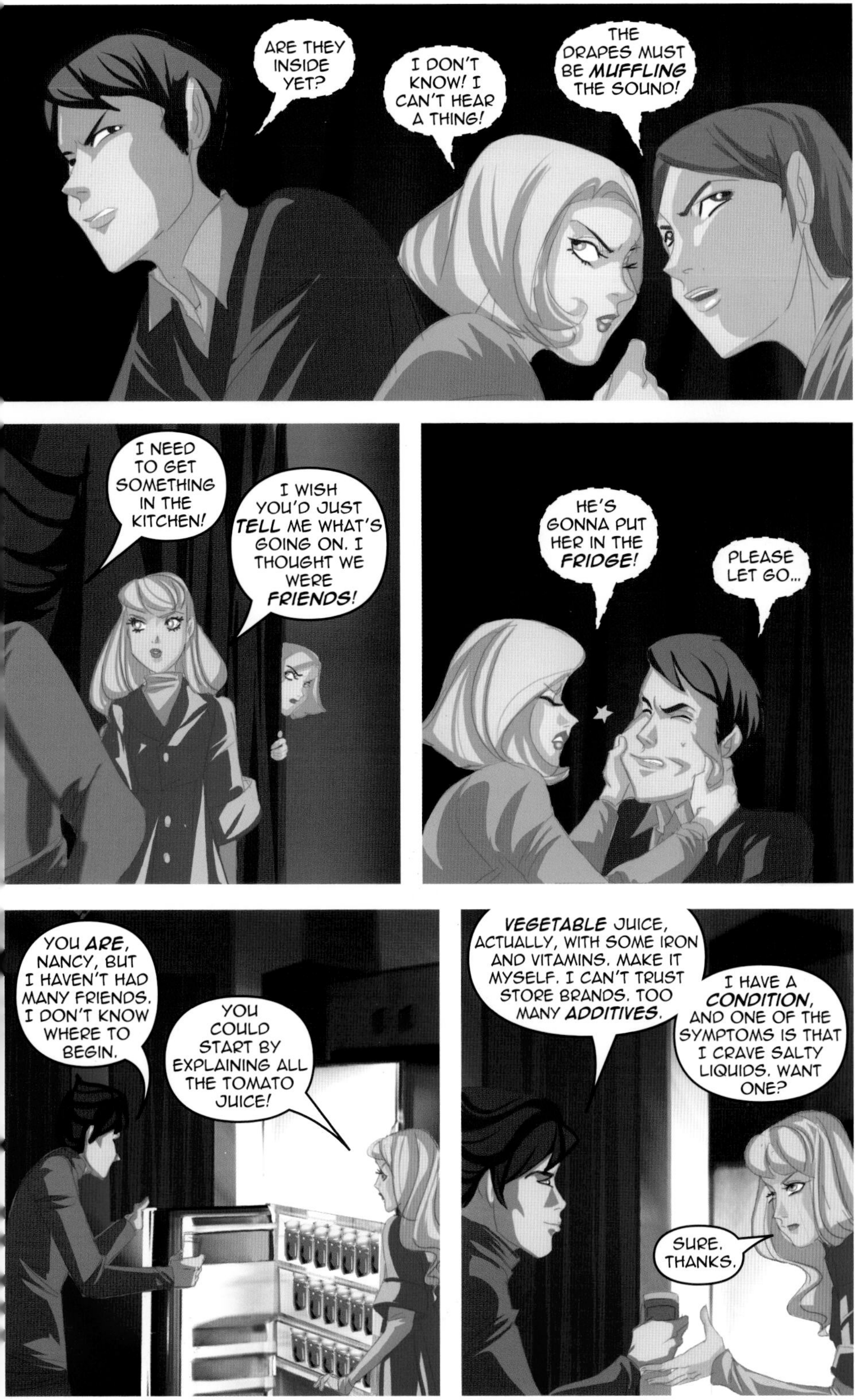
ARE THEY INSIDE YET?
I DON'T KNOW! I CAN'T HEAR A THING!
THE DRAPES MUST BE MUFFLING THE SOUND!
I NEED TO GET SOMETHING IN THE KITCHEN!
I WISH YOU'D JUST TELL ME WHAT'S GOING ON. I THOUGHT WE WERE FRIENDS!
HE'S GONNA PUT HER IN THE FRIDGE!
PLEASE LET GO...
YOU ARE, NANCY, BUT I HAVEN'T HAD MANY FRIENDS. I DON'T KNOW WHERE TO BEGIN.
YOU COULD START BY EXPLAINING ALL THE TOMATO JUICE!
VEGETABLE JUICE, ACTUALLY, WITH SOME IRON AND VITAMINS. MAKE IT MYSELF. I CAN'T TRUST STORE BRANDS. TOO MANY ADDITIVES.
I HAVE A CONDITION, AND ONE OF THE SYMPTOMS IS THAT I CRAVE SALTY LIQUIDS. WANT ONE?
SURE. THANKS.

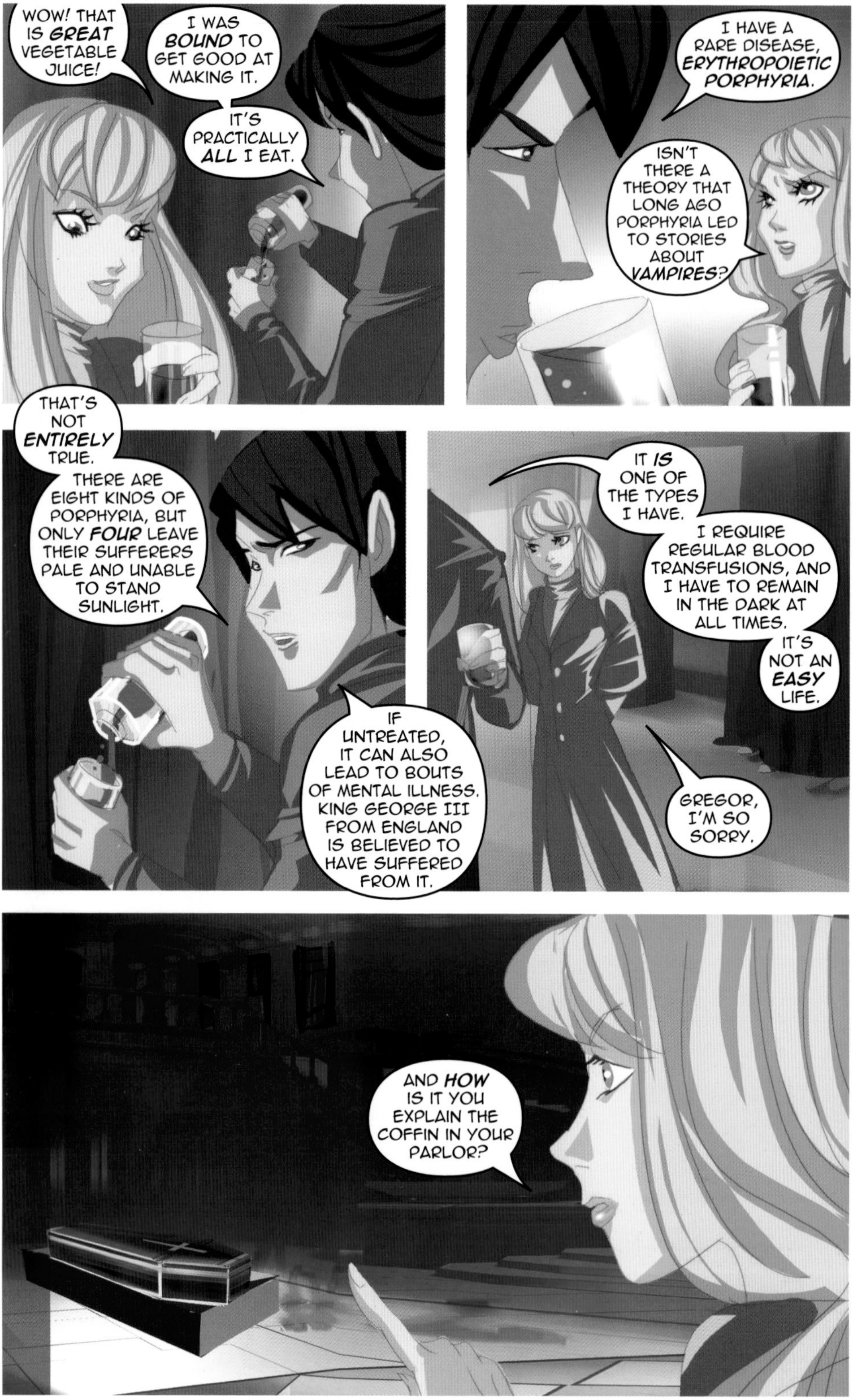
WOW! THAT IS GREAT VEGETABLE JUICE!
I WAS BOUND TO GET GOOD AT MAKING IT.
IT'S PRACTICALLY ALL I EAT.
I HAVE A RARE DISEASE, ERYTHROPOIETIC PORPHYRIA.
ISN'T THERE A THEORY THAT LONG AGO PORPHYRIA LED TO STORIES ABOUT VAMPIRES?
THAT'S NOT ENTIRELY TRUE.
THERE ARE EIGHT KINDS OF PORPHYRIA, BUT ONLY FOUR LEAVE THEIR SUFFERERS PALE AND UNABLE TO STAND SUNLIGHT.
IF UNTREATED, IT CAN ALSO LEAD TO BOUTS OF MENTAL ILLNESS. KING GEORGE III FROM ENGLAND IS BELIEVED TO HAVE SUFFERED FROM IT.
IT IS ONE OF THE TYPES I HAVE.
I REQUIRE REGULAR BLOOD TRANSFUSIONS, AND I HAVE TO REMAIN IN THE DARK AT ALL TIMES.
IT'S NOT AN EASY LIFE.
GREGOR, I'M SO SORRY.
AND HOW IS IT YOU EXPLAIN THE COFFIN IN YOUR PARLOR?

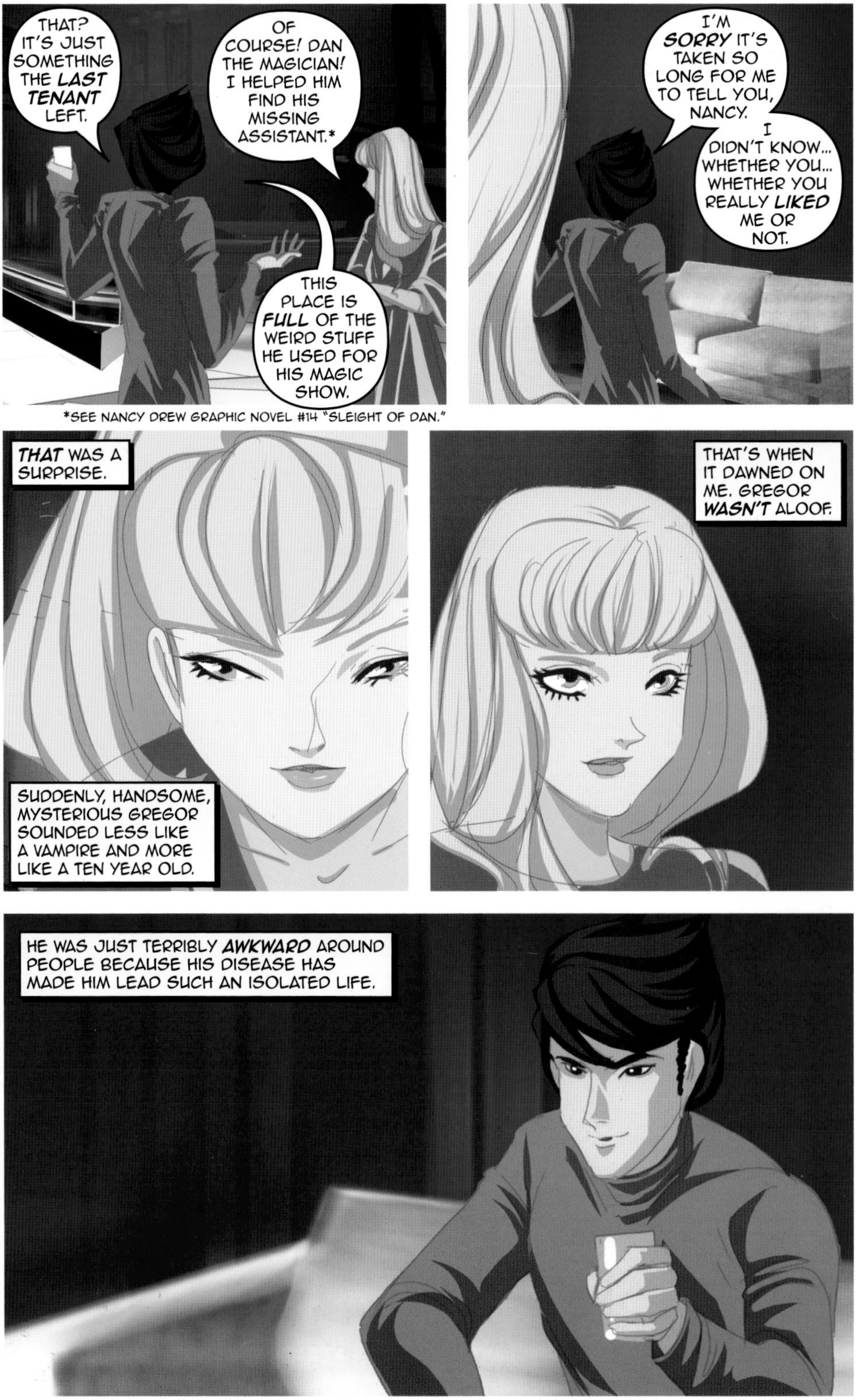
THAT? IT'S JUST SOMETHING THE LAST TENANT LEFT.
OF COURSE! DAN THE MAGICIAN! I HELPED HIM FIND HIS MISSING ASSISTANT.*
THIS PLACE IS FULL OF THE WEIRD STUFF HE USED FOR HIS MAGIC SHOW.
I'M SORRY IT'S TAKEN SO LONG FOR ME TO TELL YOU, NANCY.
I DIDN'T KNOW... WHETHER YOU... WHETHER YOU REALLY LIKED ME OR NOT.
*SEE NANCY DREW GRAPHIC NOVEL #14 "SLEIGHT OF DAN."
THAT WAS A SURPRISE.
SUDDENLY, HANDSOME, MYSTERIOUS GREGOR SOUNDED LESS LIKE A VAMPIRE AND MORE LIKE A TEN YEAR OLD.
THAT'S WHEN IT DAWNED ON ME. GREGOR WASN'T ALOOF.
HE WAS JUST TERRIBLY AWKWARD AROUND PEOPLE BECAUSE HIS DISEASE HAS MADE HIM LEAD SUCH AN ISOLATED LIFE.

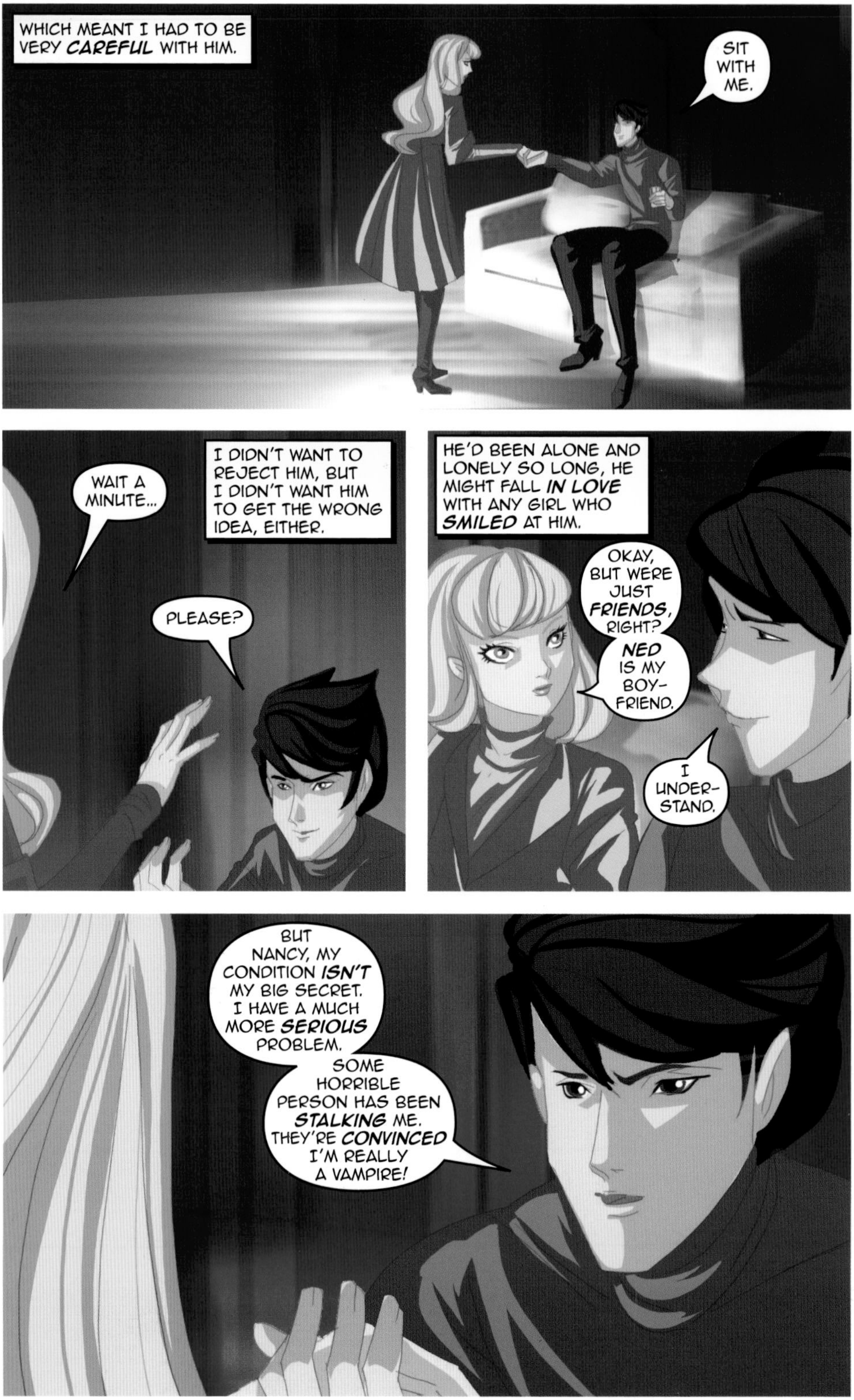
WHICH MEANT I HAD TO BE VERY CAREFUL WITH HIM.
SIT WITH ME.
WAIT A MINUTE...
I DIDN'T WANT TO REJECT HIM, BUT I DIDN'T WANT HIM TO GET THE WRONG IDEA, EITHER.
PLEASE?
HE'D BEEN ALONE AND LONELY SO LONG, HE MIGHT FALL IN LOVE WITH ANY GIRL WHO SMILED AT HIM.
OKAY, BUT WERE JUST FRIENDS, RIGHT?
NED IS MY BOY-FRIEND.
I UNDER-STAND.
BUT NANCY, MY CONDITION ISN'T MY BIG SECRET. I HAVE A MUCH MORE SERIOUS PROBLEM.
SOME HORRIBLE PERSON HAS BEEN STALKING ME. THEY'RE CONVINCED I'M REALLY A VAMPIRE!

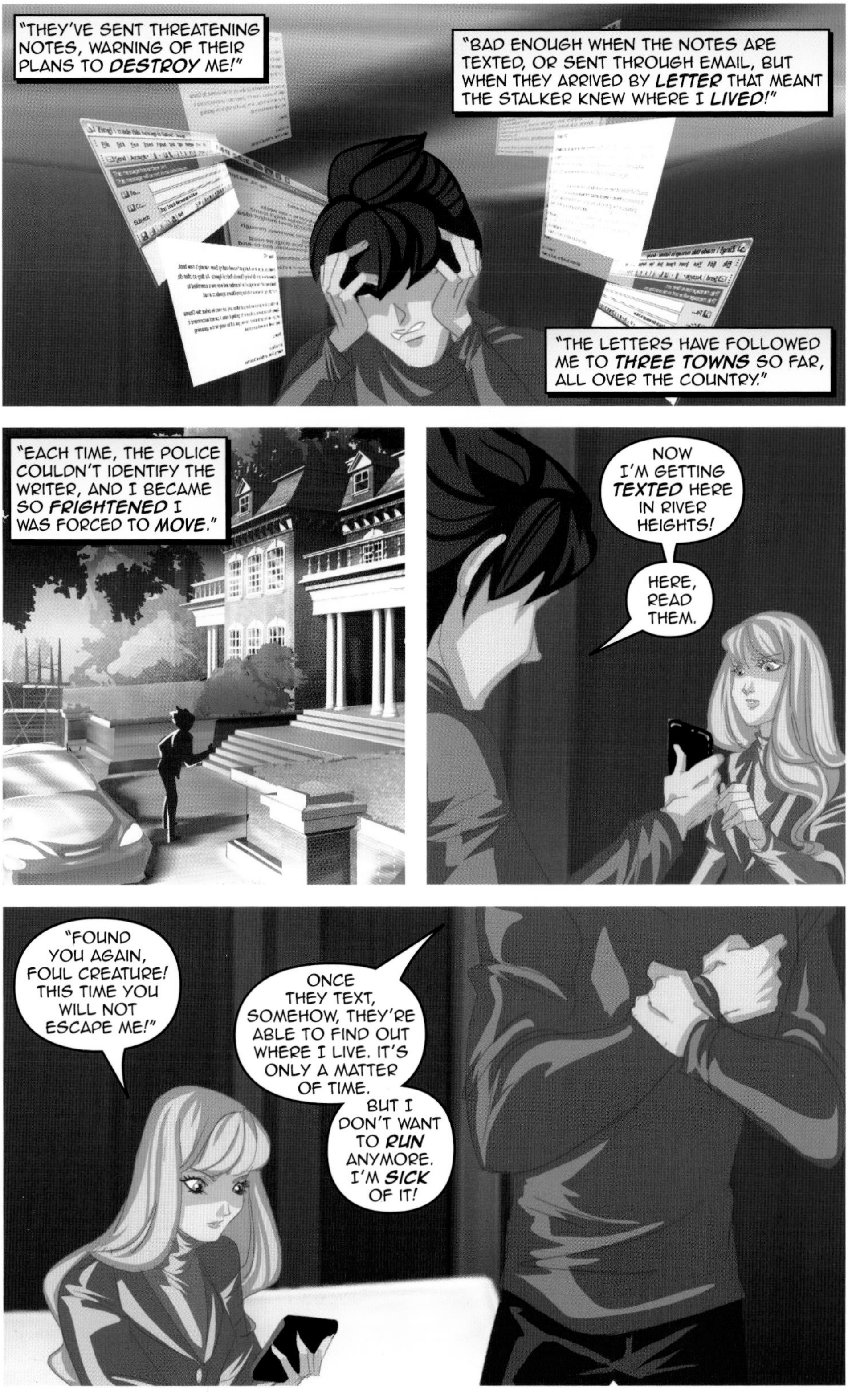
"THEY'VE SENT THREATENING NOTES, WARNING OF THEIR PLANS TO *DESTROY* ME!"
"BAD ENOUGH WHEN THE NOTES ARE TEXTED, OR SENT THROUGH EMAIL, BUT WHEN THEY ARRIVED BY *LETTER* THAT MEANT THE STALKER KNEW WHERE I *LIVED!*"
"THE LETTERS HAVE FOLLOWED ME TO *THREE TOWNS* SO FAR, ALL OVER THE COUNTRY."
"EACH TIME, THE POLICE COULDN'T IDENTIFY THE WRITER, AND I BECAME SO *FRIGHTENED* I WAS FORCED TO *MOVE*."
NOW I'M GETTING *TEXTED* HERE IN RIVER HEIGHTS!
HERE, READ THEM.
"FOUND YOU AGAIN, FOUL CREATURE! THIS TIME YOU WILL NOT ESCAPE ME!"
ONCE THEY TEXT, SOMEHOW, THEY'RE ABLE TO FIND OUT WHERE I LIVE. IT'S ONLY A MATTER OF TIME.
BUT I DON'T WANT TO *RUN* ANYMORE. I'M *SICK* OF IT!

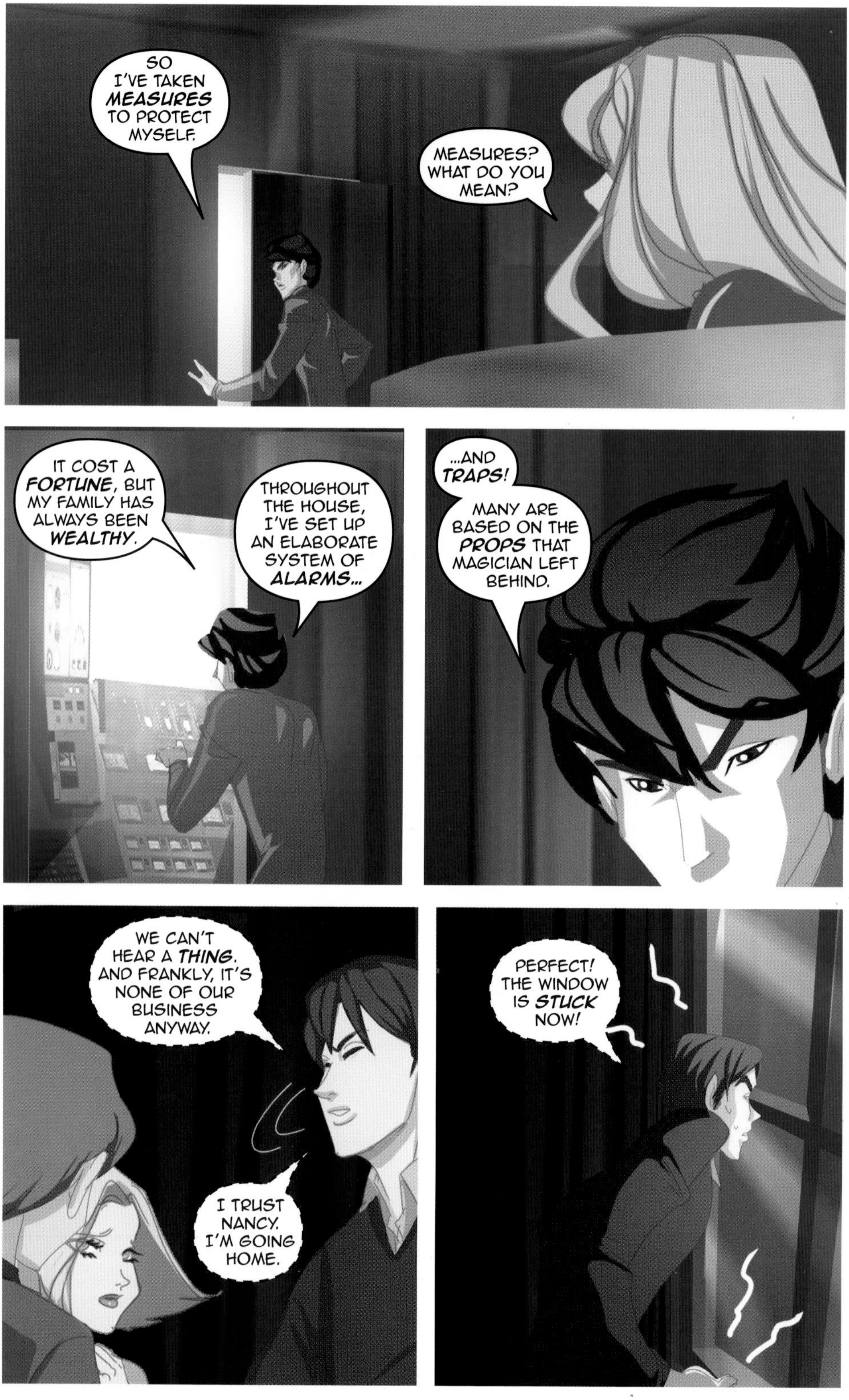
SO I'VE TAKEN MEASURES TO PROTECT MYSELF.
MEASURES? WHAT DO YOU MEAN?
IT COST A FORTUNE, BUT MY FAMILY HAS ALWAYS BEEN WEALTHY.
THROUGHOUT THE HOUSE, I'VE SET UP AN ELABORATE SYSTEM OF ALARMS...
...AND TRAPS!
MANY ARE BASED ON THE PROPS THAT MAGICIAN LEFT BEHIND.
WE CAN'T HEAR A THING. AND FRANKLY, IT'S NONE OF OUR BUSINESS ANYWAY.
I TRUST NANCY. I'M GOING HOME.
PERFECT! THE WINDOW IS STUCK NOW!

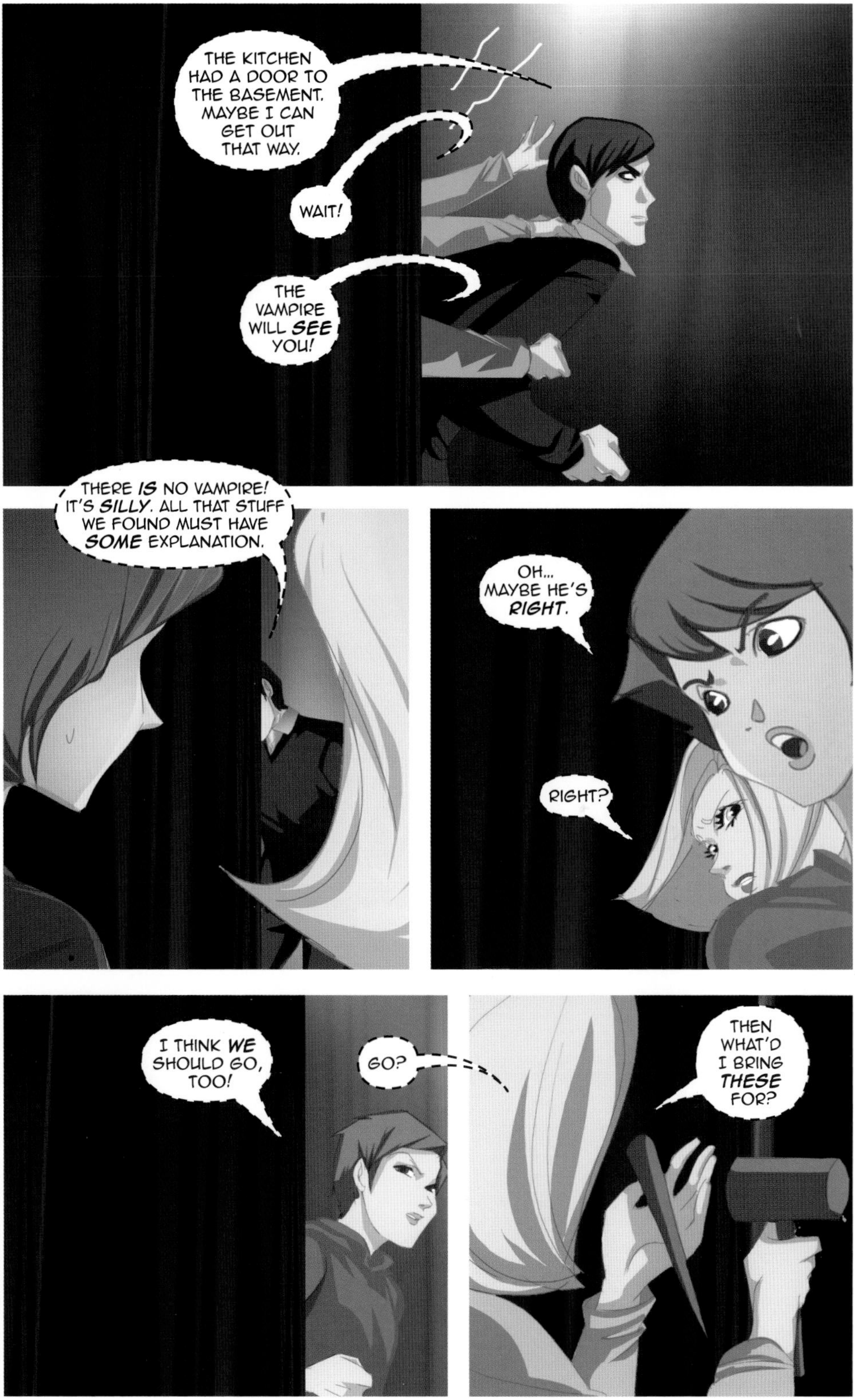

THE KITCHEN HAD A DOOR TO THE BASEMENT. MAYBE I CAN GET OUT THAT WAY.
WAIT!
THE VAMPIRE WILL SEE YOU!
THERE IS NO VAMPIRE! IT'S SILLY. ALL THAT STUFF WE FOUND MUST HAVE SOME EXPLANATION.
OH... MAYBE HE'S RIGHT.
RIGHT?
I THINK WE SHOULD GO, TOO!
GO?
THEN WHAT'D I BRING THESE FOR?

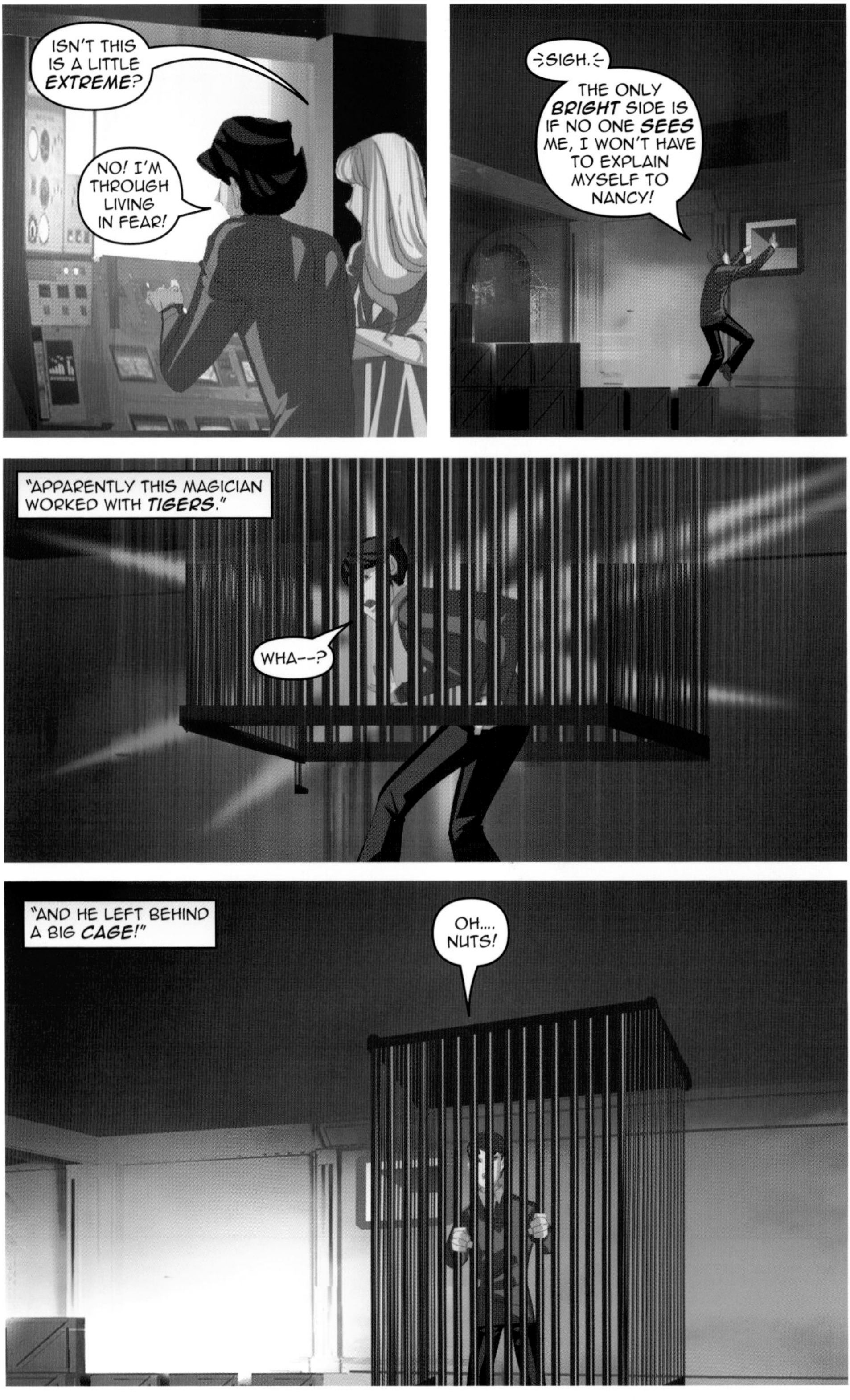
ISN'T THIS IS A LITTLE EXTREME?
NO! I'M THROUGH LIVING IN FEAR!
SIGH.
THE ONLY BRIGHT SIDE IS IF NO ONE SEES ME, I WON'T HAVE TO EXPLAIN MYSELF TO NANCY!
"APPARENTLY THIS MAGICIAN WORKED WITH TIGERS."
WHA--?
"AND HE LEFT BEHIND A BIG CAGE!"
OH.... NUTS!

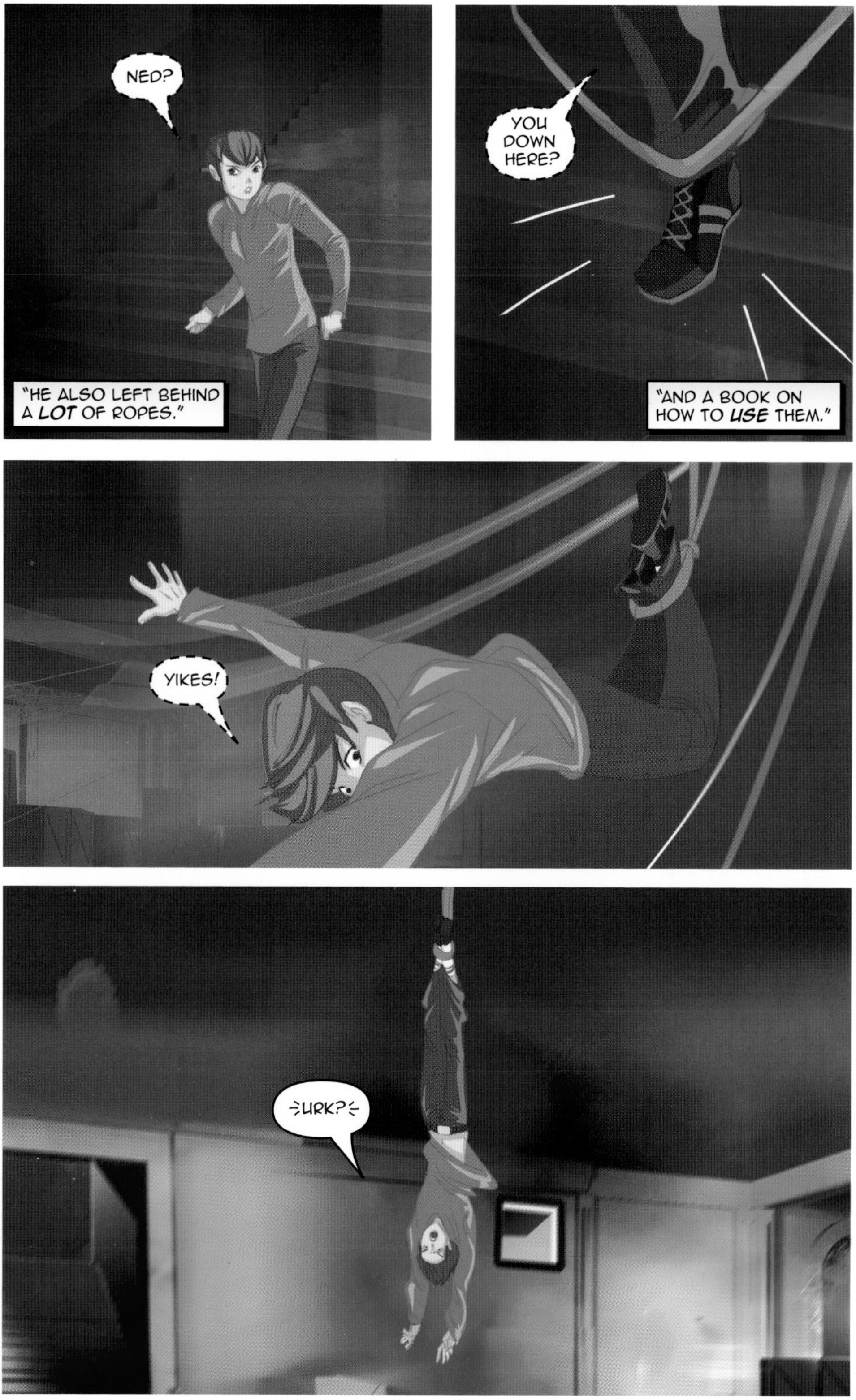
NED?
"HE ALSO LEFT BEHIND A **LOT** OF ROPES."
YOU DOWN HERE?
"AND A BOOK ON HOW TO **USE** THEM."
YIKES!
URK?

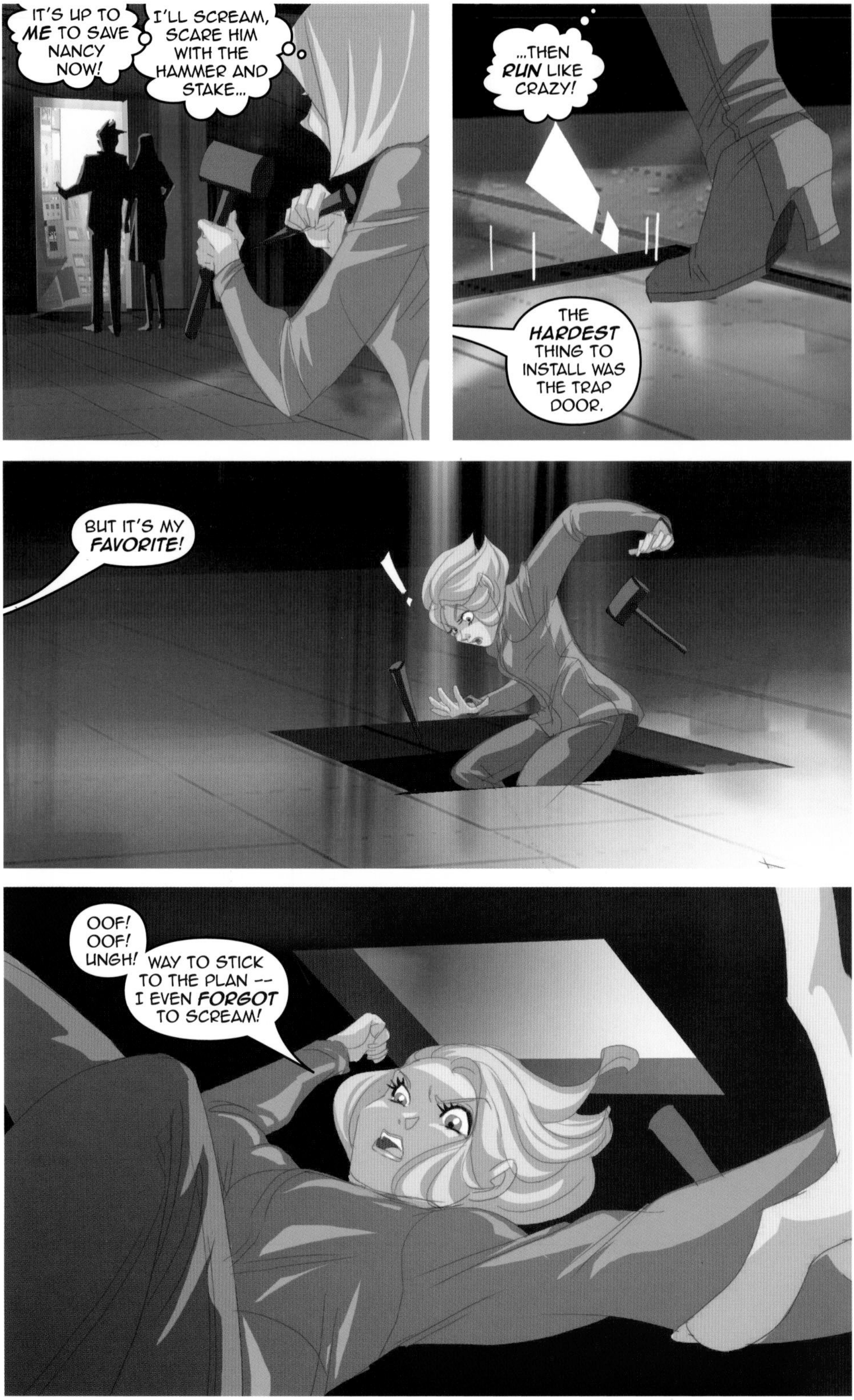

IT'S UP TO ME TO SAVE NANCY NOW!
I'LL SCREAM, SCARE HIM WITH THE HAMMER AND STAKE...
...THEN RUN LIKE CRAZY!
THE HARDEST THING TO INSTALL WAS THE TRAP DOOR.
BUT IT'S MY FAVORITE!
!
OOF! OOF! UNGH!
WAY TO STICK TO THE PLAN -- I EVEN FORGOT TO SCREAM!

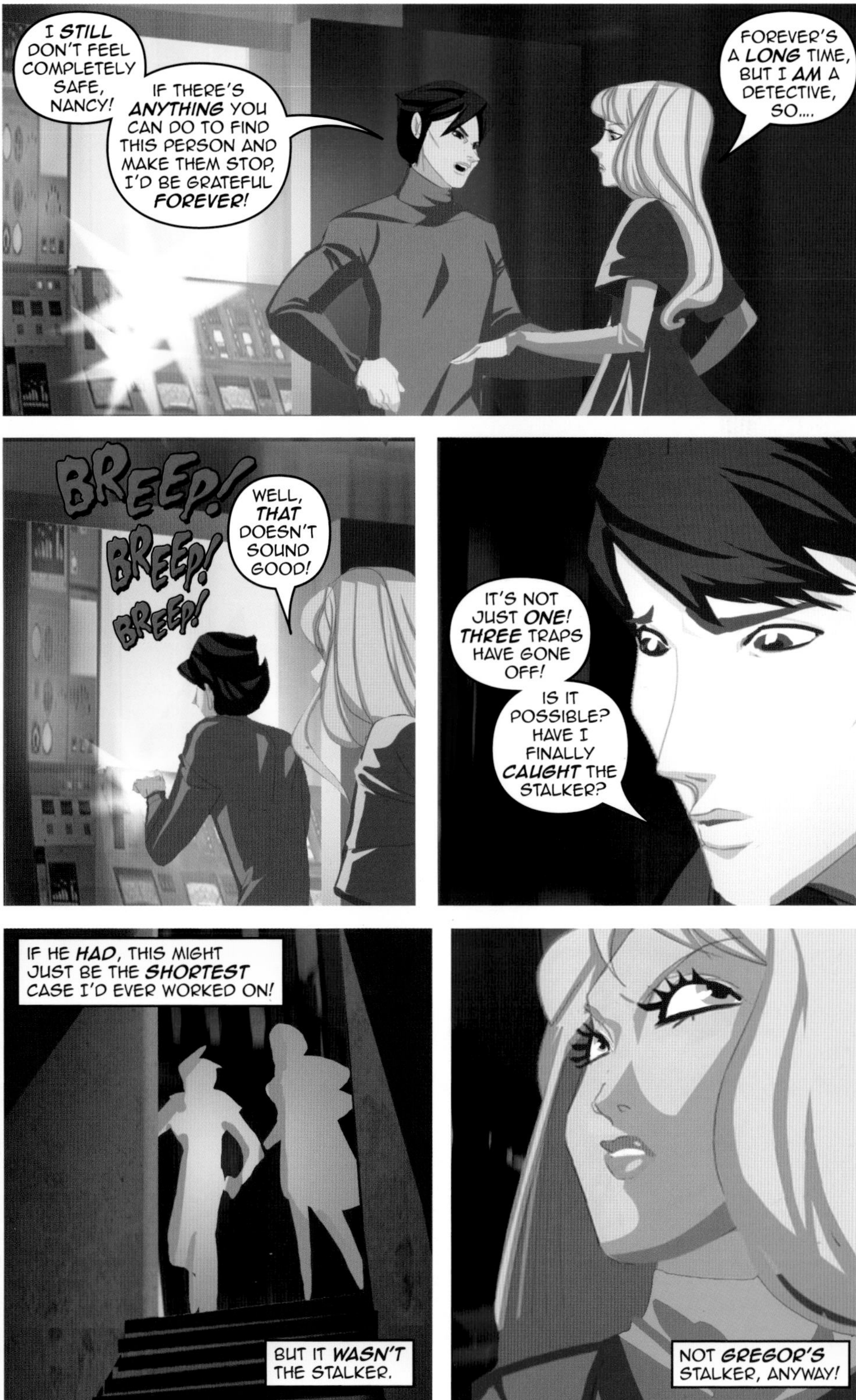
I STILL DON'T FEEL COMPLETELY SAFE, NANCY!
IF THERE'S ANYTHING YOU CAN DO TO FIND THIS PERSON AND MAKE THEM STOP, I'D BE GRATEFUL FOREVER!
FOREVER'S A LONG TIME, BUT I AM A DETECTIVE, SO....
BREEP! BREEP! BREEP!
WELL, THAT DOESN'T SOUND GOOD!
IT'S NOT JUST ONE! THREE TRAPS HAVE GONE OFF!
IS IT POSSIBLE? HAVE I FINALLY CAUGHT THE STALKER?
IF HE HAD, THIS MIGHT JUST BE THE SHORTEST CASE I'D EVER WORKED ON!
BUT IT WASN'T THE STALKER.
NOT GREGOR'S STALKER, ANYWAY!

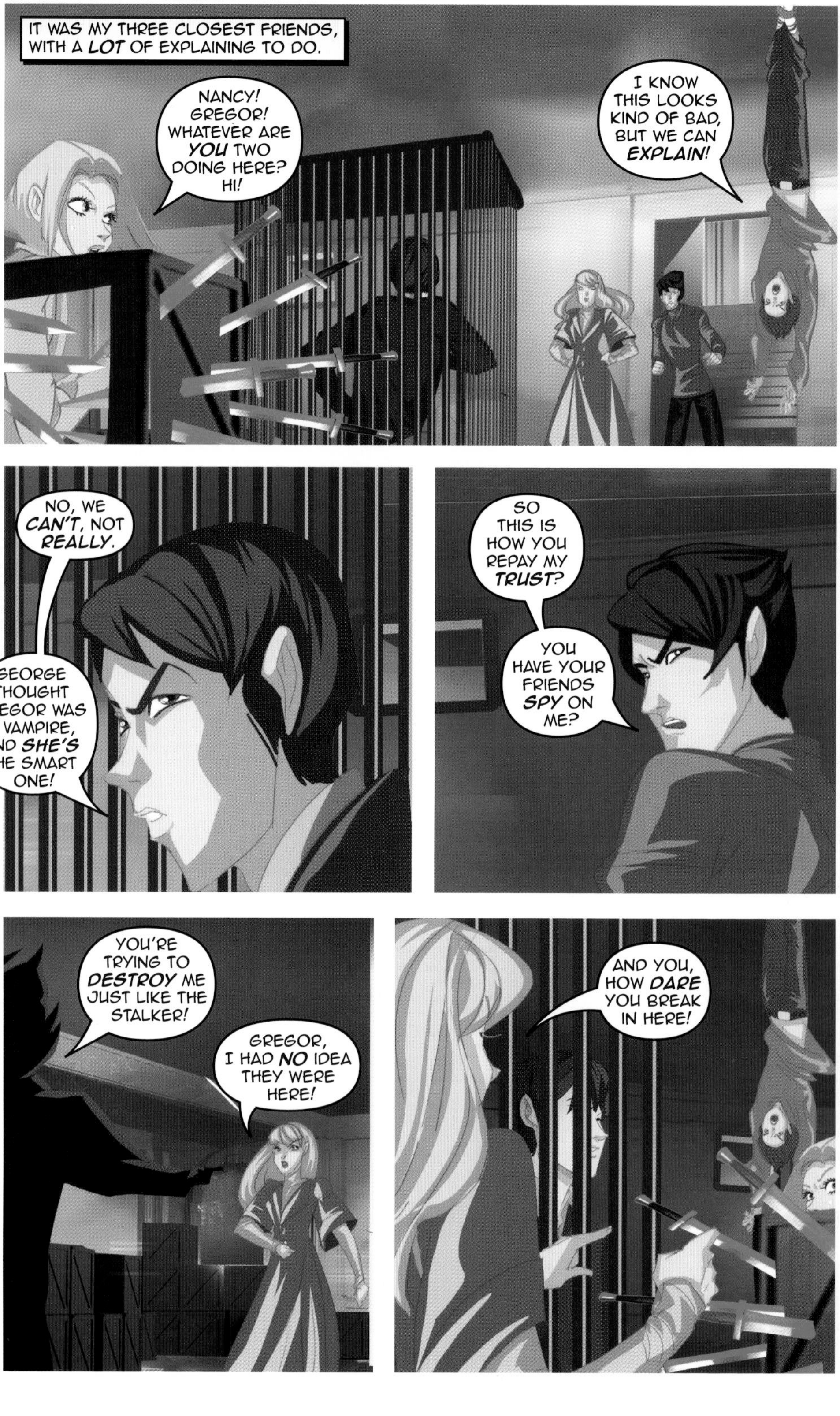
IT WAS MY THREE CLOSEST FRIENDS, WITH A LOT OF EXPLAINING TO DO.
NANCY! GREGOR! WHATEVER ARE YOU TWO DOING HERE? HI!
I KNOW THIS LOOKS KIND OF BAD, BUT WE CAN EXPLAIN!
NO, WE CAN'T, NOT REALLY.
GEORGE THOUGHT GREGOR WAS A VAMPIRE, AND SHE'S THE SMART ONE!
SO THIS IS HOW YOU REPAY MY TRUST?
YOU HAVE YOUR FRIENDS SPY ON ME?
YOU'RE TRYING TO DESTROY ME JUST LIKE THE STALKER!
GREGOR, I HAD NO IDEA THEY WERE HERE!
AND YOU, HOW DARE YOU BREAK IN HERE!

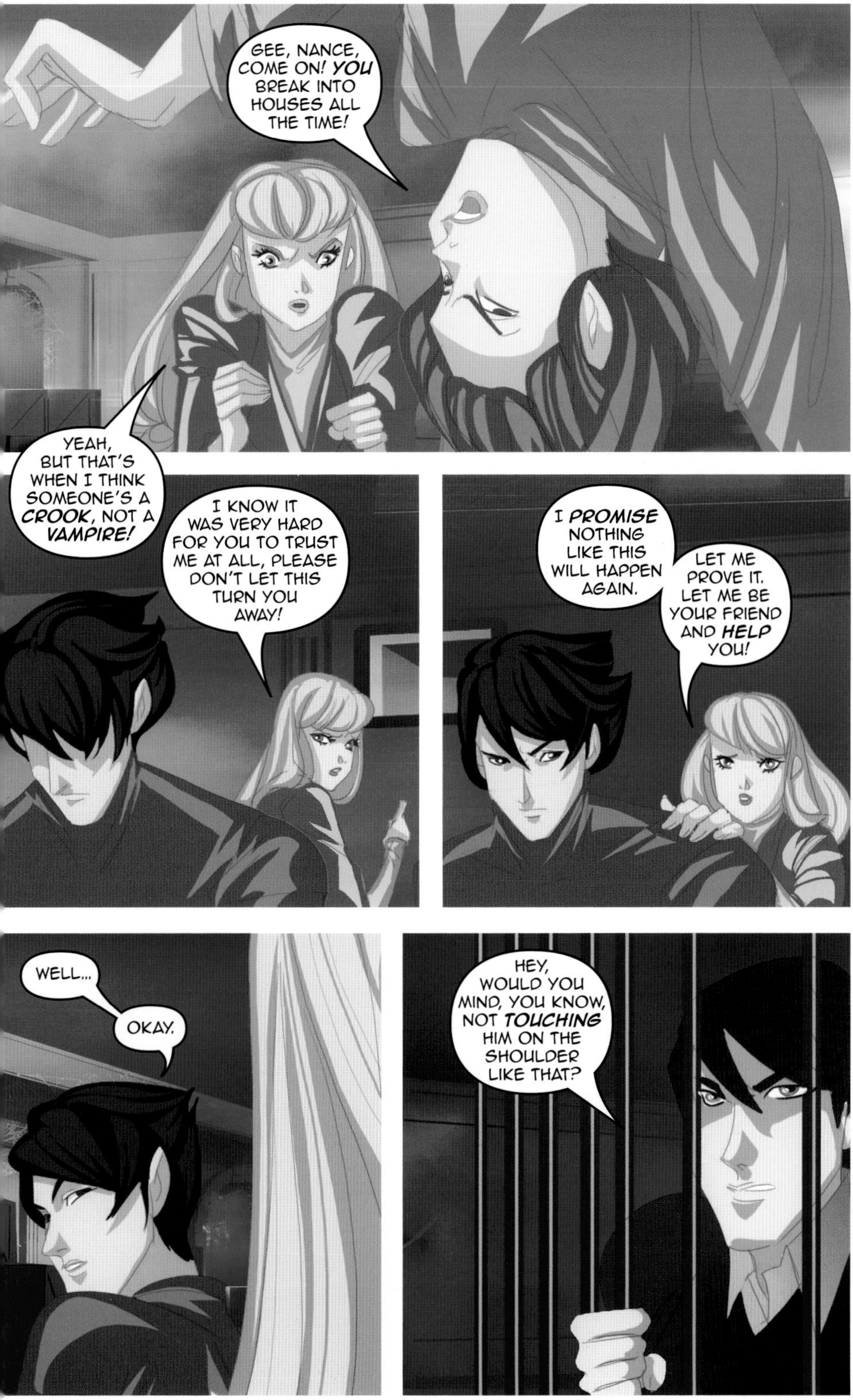
GEE, NANCE, COME ON! *YOU* BREAK INTO HOUSES ALL THE TIME!
YEAH, BUT THAT'S WHEN I THINK SOMEONE'S A *CROOK*, NOT A *VAMPIRE!*
I KNOW IT WAS VERY HARD FOR YOU TO TRUST ME AT ALL, PLEASE DON'T LET THIS TURN YOU AWAY!
I *PROMISE* NOTHING LIKE THIS WILL HAPPEN AGAIN.
LET ME PROVE IT. LET ME BE YOUR FRIEND AND *HELP* YOU!
WELL...
OKAY.
HEY, WOULD YOU MIND, YOU KNOW, NOT *TOUCHING* HIM ON THE SHOULDER LIKE THAT?

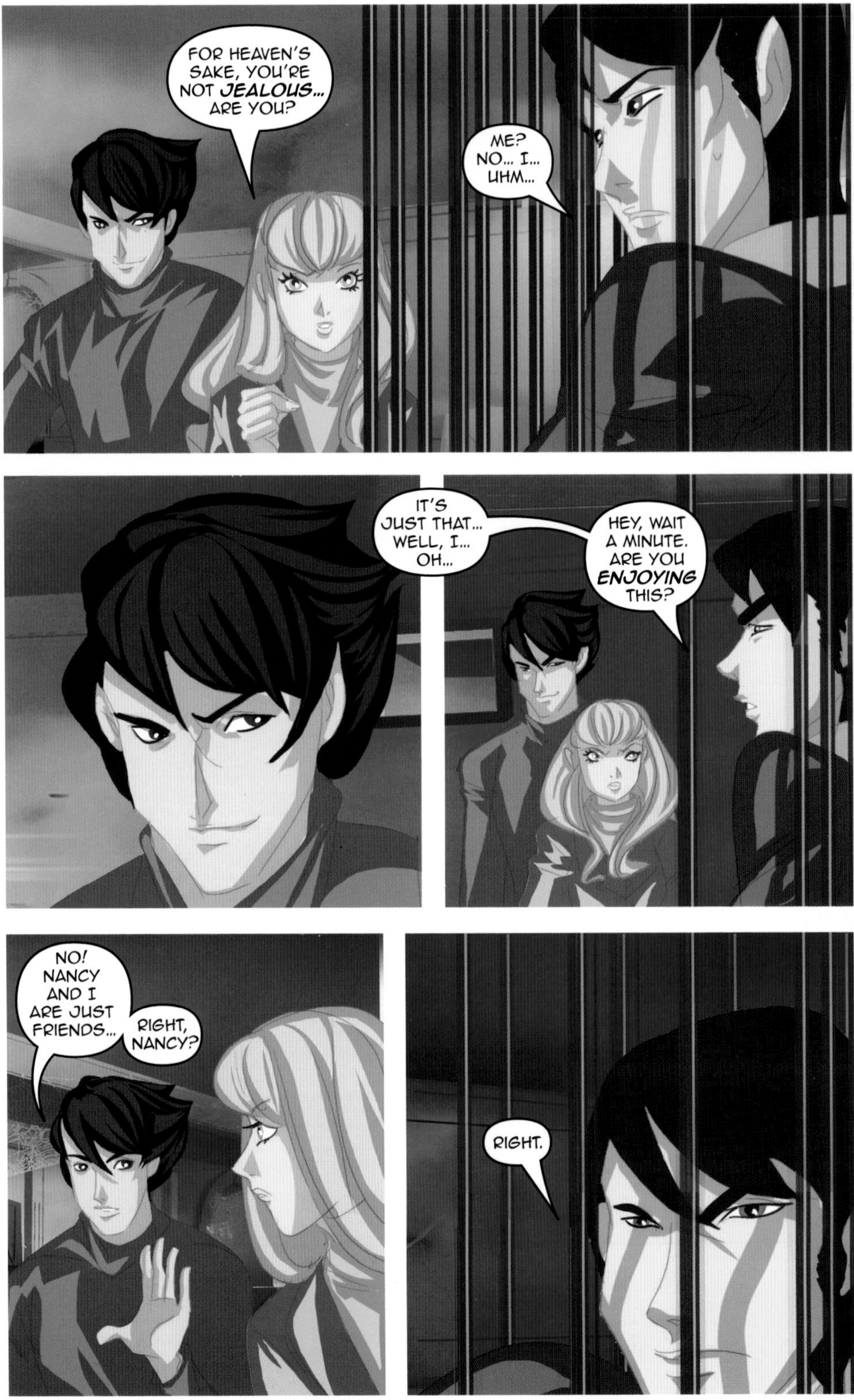
FOR HEAVEN'S SAKE, YOU'RE NOT JEALOUS... ARE YOU?
ME? NO... I... UHM...
IT'S JUST THAT... WELL, I... OH...
HEY, WAIT A MINUTE. ARE YOU ENJOYING THIS?
NO! NANCY AND I ARE JUST FRIENDS...
RIGHT, NANCY?
RIGHT.

BUT IF YOU REALLY WANT ME TO TRUST YOU, LIKE YOU SAY...

...THEN YOU'LL TELL YOUR FRIENDS TO LEAVE *NOW!*

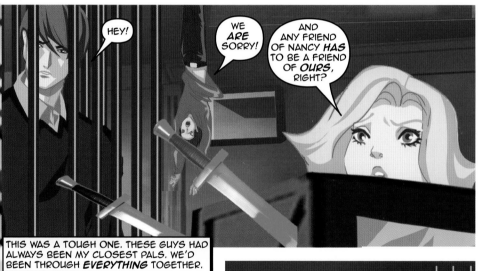

HEY!

WE *ARE* SORRY!

AND ANY FRIEND OF NANCY *HAS* TO BE A FRIEND OF *OURS*, RIGHT?

THIS WAS A TOUGH ONE. THESE GUYS HAD ALWAYS BEEN MY CLOSEST PALS. WE'D BEEN THROUGH *EVERYTHING* TOGETHER.

BUT CLEARLY *THEY* DIDN'T TRUST ME, AND GREGOR WAS VERY SKITTISH TO BEGIN WITH, SO...

NO. I'M SORRY, BUT YOU'VE GOT TO *LEAVE* GREGOR'S HOUSE.

NOW.

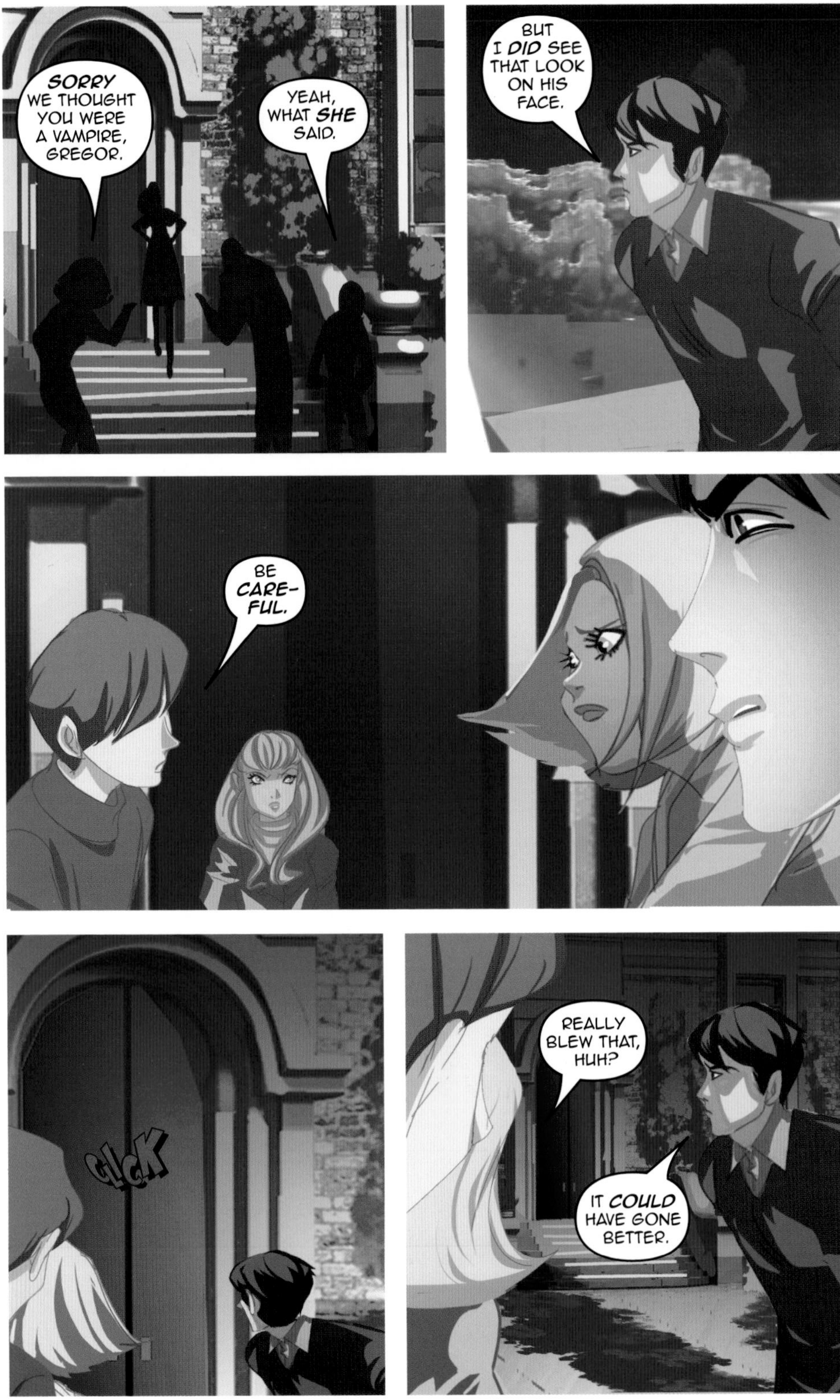
SORRY WE THOUGHT YOU WERE A VAMPIRE, GREGOR.
YEAH, WHAT SHE SAID.
BUT I DID SEE THAT LOOK ON HIS FACE.
BE CARE-FUL.
CLICK
REALLY BLEW THAT, HUH?
IT COULD HAVE GONE BETTER.

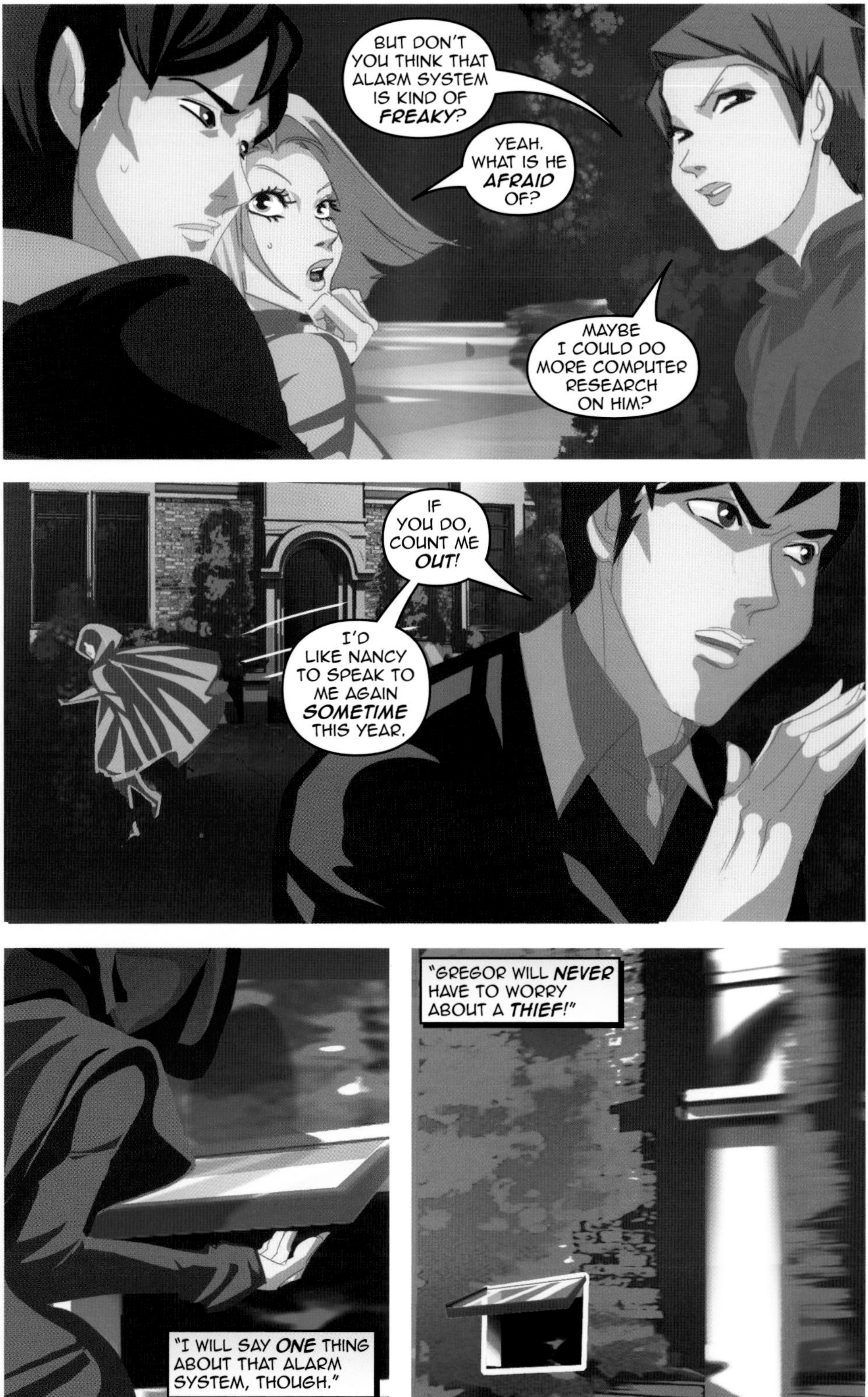

BUT DON'T YOU THINK THAT ALARM SYSTEM IS KIND OF FREAKY?
YEAH. WHAT IS HE AFRAID OF?
MAYBE I COULD DO MORE COMPUTER RESEARCH ON HIM?
IF YOU DO, COUNT ME OUT!
I'D LIKE NANCY TO SPEAK TO ME AGAIN SOMETIME THIS YEAR.
"I WILL SAY ONE THING ABOUT THAT ALARM SYSTEM, THOUGH."
"GREGOR WILL NEVER HAVE TO WORRY ABOUT A THIEF!"

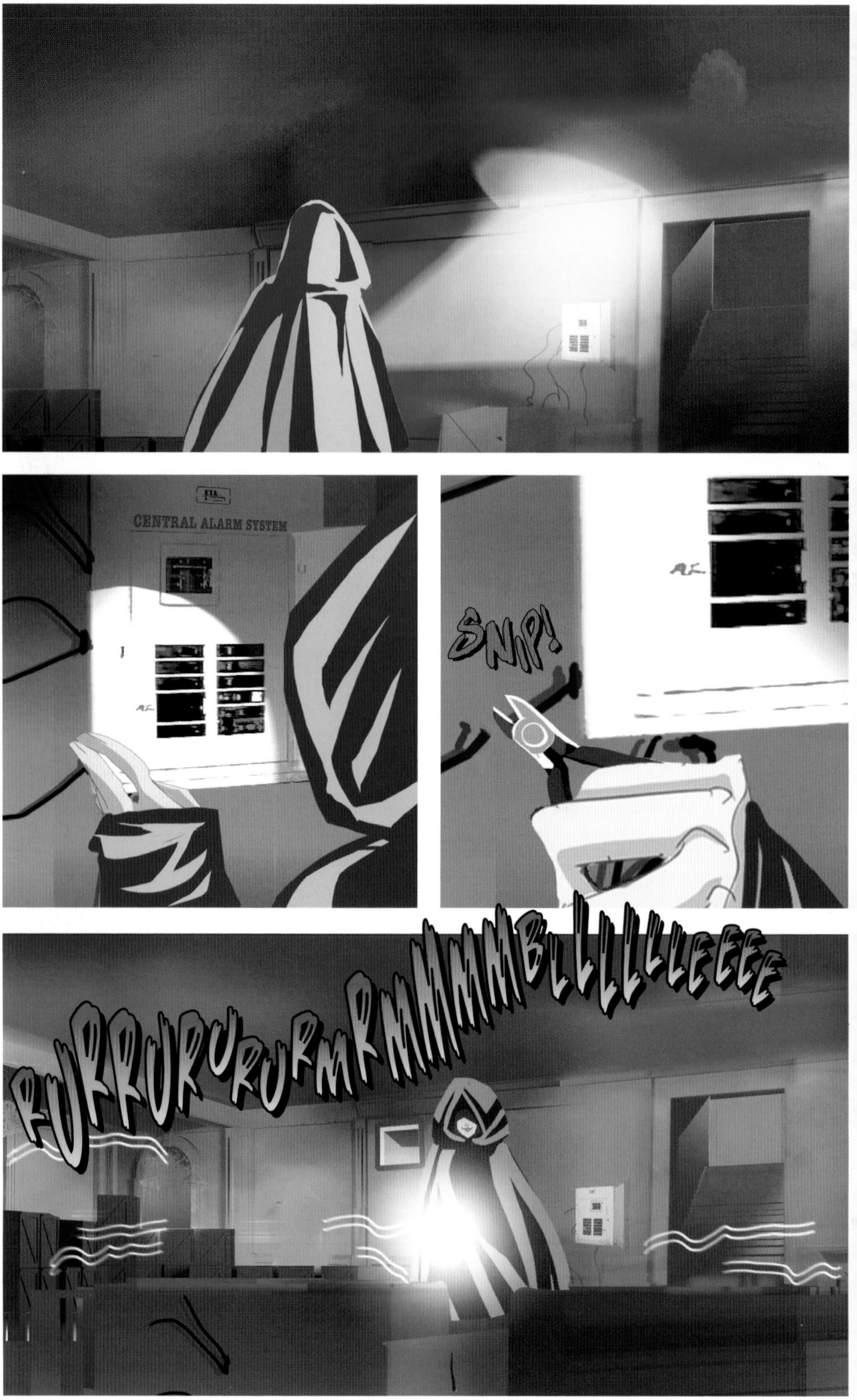
CENTRAL ALARM SYSTEM
SNIP!
RURRURURURMRMMMMMBLLLLLLEEE

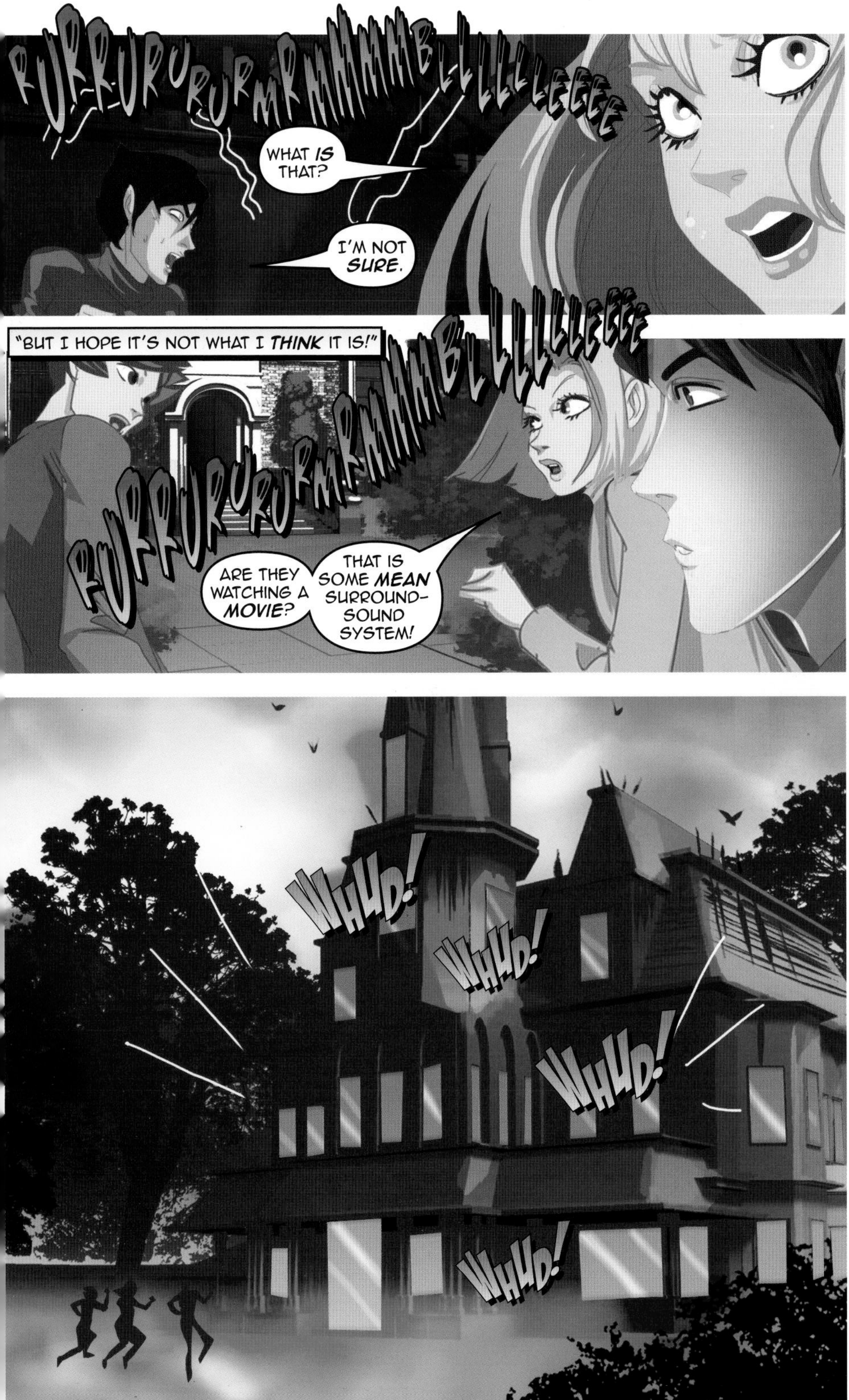
RURRURURURMRMMMMBLLLLLLEEEE
WHAT IS THAT?
I'M NOT SURE.
"BUT I HOPE IT'S NOT WHAT I THINK IT IS!"
RURRURURURMRMMMBLLLLLLEEEE
ARE THEY WATCHING A MOVIE?
THAT IS SOME MEAN SURROUND-SOUND SYSTEM!
WHUD!
WHUD!
WHUD!
WHUD!

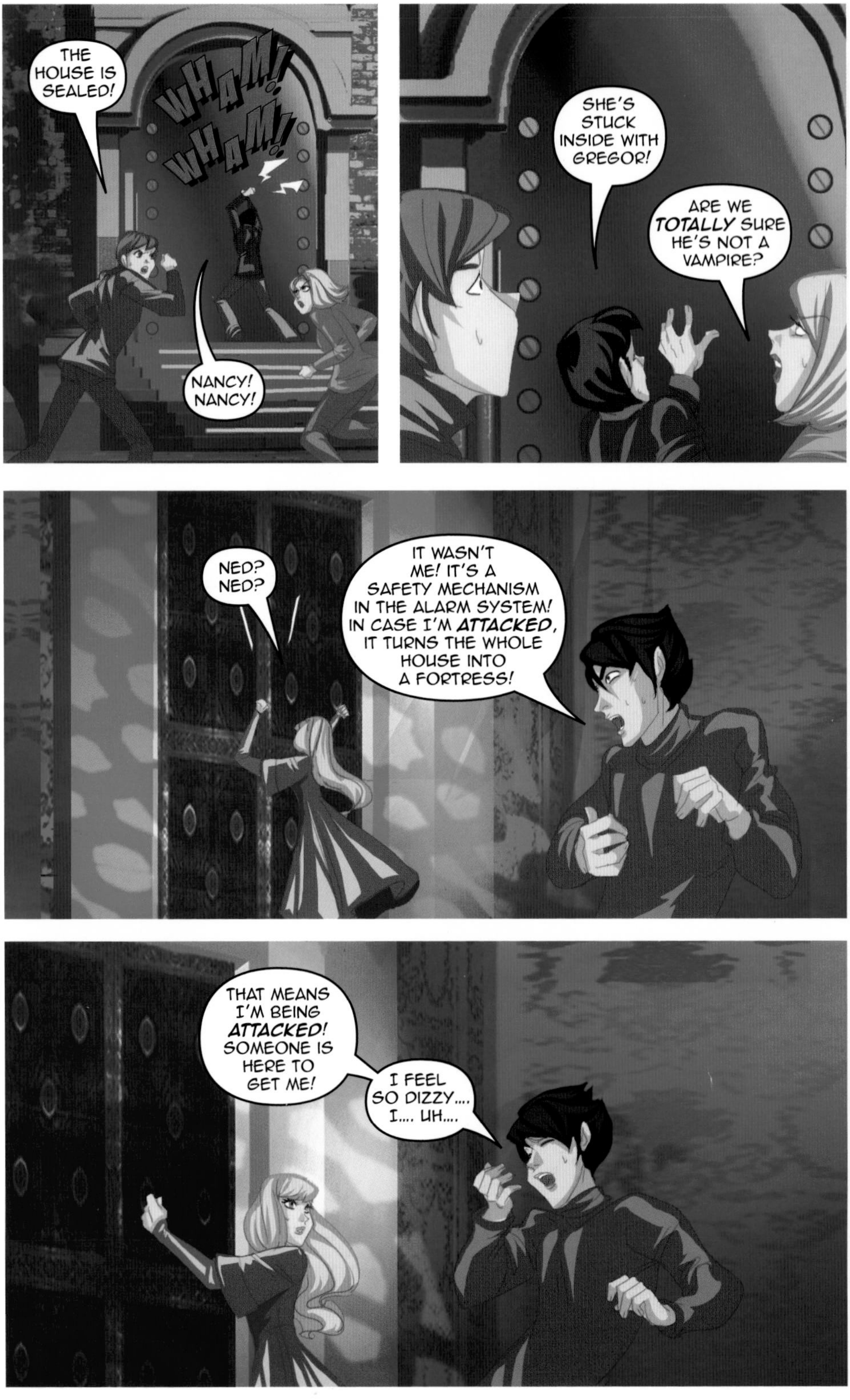
THE HOUSE IS SEALED!
WHAM! WHAM!
NANCY! NANCY!
SHE'S STUCK INSIDE WITH GREGOR!
ARE WE TOTALLY SURE HE'S NOT A VAMPIRE?
NED? NED?
IT WASN'T ME! IT'S A SAFETY MECHANISM IN THE ALARM SYSTEM! IN CASE I'M ATTACKED, IT TURNS THE WHOLE HOUSE INTO A FORTRESS!
THAT MEANS I'M BEING ATTACKED! SOMEONE IS HERE TO GET ME!
I FEEL SO DIZZY.... I.... UH....

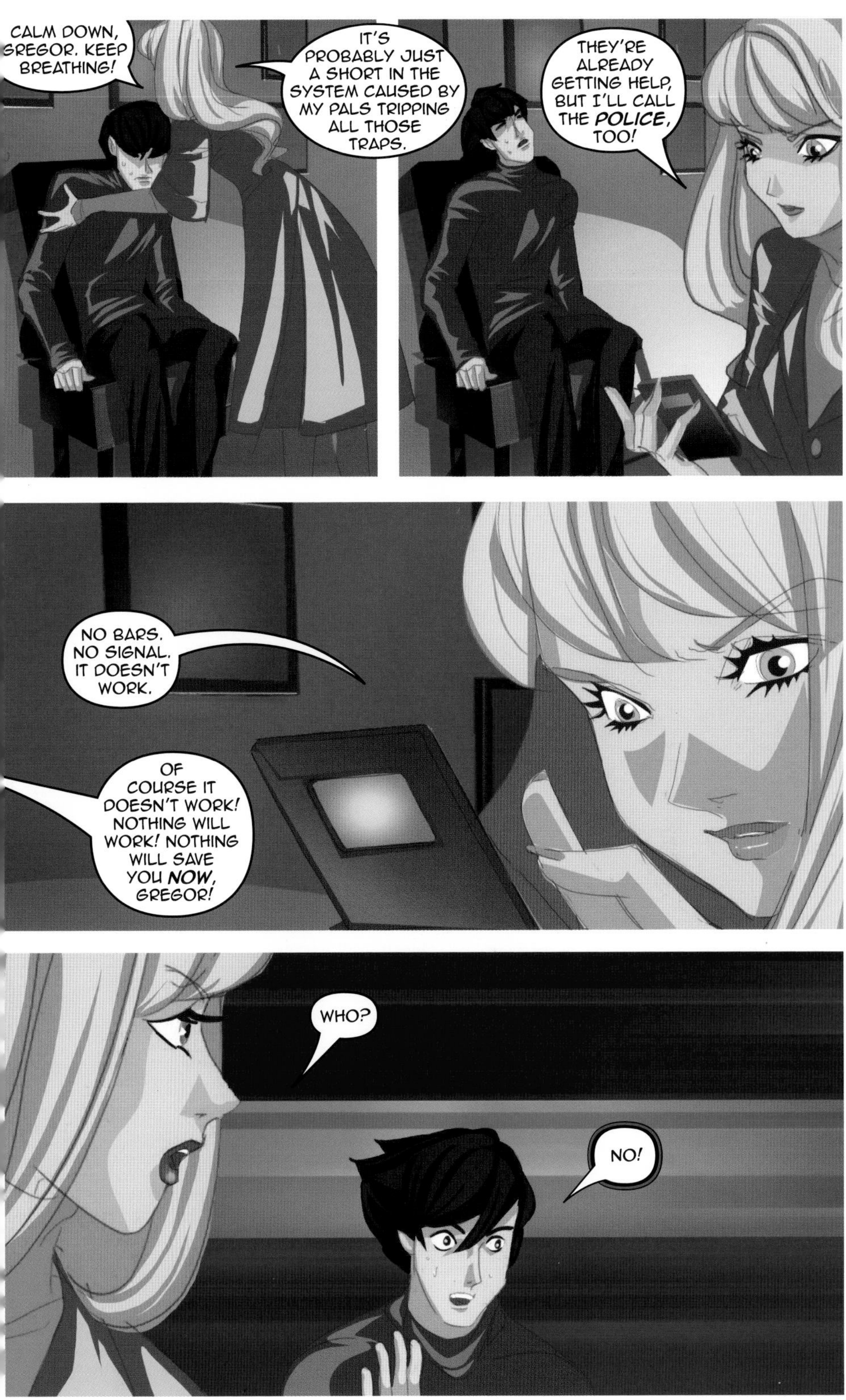
CALM DOWN, GREGOR. KEEP BREATHING!
IT'S PROBABLY JUST A SHORT IN THE SYSTEM CAUSED BY MY PALS TRIPPING ALL THOSE TRAPS.
THEY'RE ALREADY GETTING HELP, BUT I'LL CALL THE *POLICE*, TOO!
NO BARS. NO SIGNAL. IT DOESN'T WORK.
OF COURSE IT DOESN'T WORK! NOTHING WILL WORK! NOTHING WILL SAVE YOU *NOW*, GREGOR!
WHO?
NO!

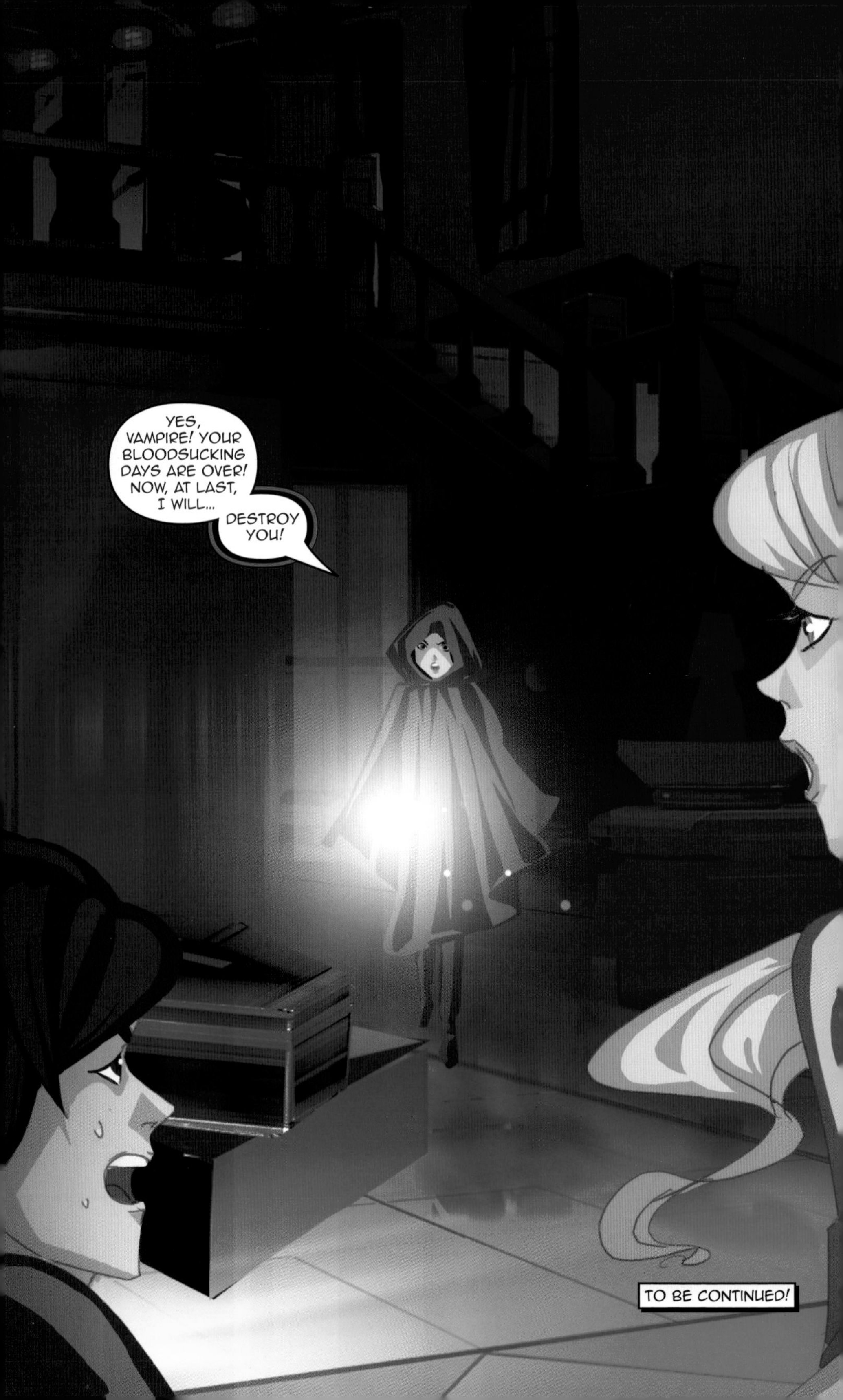
YES, VAMPIRE! YOUR BLOODSUCKING DAYS ARE OVER! NOW, AT LAST, I WILL...
DESTROY YOU!
TO BE CONTINUED!

WATCH OUT FOR PAPERCUTZ™

Welcome to the premiere edition of the all-new NANCY DREW graphic novel series! I'm Jim Salicrup, Editor-in-Chief of Papercutz, publisher of graphic novels for all-ages. If you were a follower of Nancy's first graphic novel series, welcome back! If you're new to Nancy Drew in comics form, well, you're in for a real treat! Nancy Drew is just as fun and exciting in comics form as she is in her prose series.

In fact, we strive to preserve all the wonderful things that have made Nancy Drew so popular and successful in her book series in our all-new graphic novel stories. Artist Sho Murase and Carlos Guzman do an amazing job of bringing Nancy, Bess, George, Ned, and the rest to comics life. Many people have said that our NANCY DREW graphic novels are like seeing an animated movie on paper! Writers Stefan Petrucha and Sarah Kinney are always finding challenging new mysteries for the world famous Girl Detective, and considering that 2010 is the 80th anniversary of Nancy Drew that is no easy task! Nancy has virtually done it all! But she's never met a vampire before… or has she?

Years ago, Nancy, along with The Hardy Boys, shared a prime time network TV series on ABC. If you track down a DVD of the second season opener of "The Hardy Boys/Nancy Drew Mysteries" series from September 11 and 18 1977 you'll find the two-part episode "The Hardy Boys and Nancy Drew Meet Dracula"! Was he really Dracula? Who knows?

And what about Nancy Drew becoming a "vampire slayer"..? Crazy idea? Well, we know of one vampire who may not think so-- in season 4, episode 21 of "Buffy the Vampire Slayer," Spike, a vampire, looks at Buffy and says "Look at little Nancy Drew."

If you're one of those people new to the NANCY DREW graphic novels, and you're looking to find more NANCY DREW graphic novels to enjoy, let me direct your attention to page two. You'll find lots of wonderful NANCY DREW graphic novels to choose from. They're available at booksellers everywhere, but if your favorite bookseller is out of stock, you can always order directly from us—but we suggest trying bookstores and online booksellers first. And if you're already a fan of NANCY DREW graphic novels, you can order any of the books you're missing! Who doesn't want a complete collection of NANCY DREW graphic novels after all?

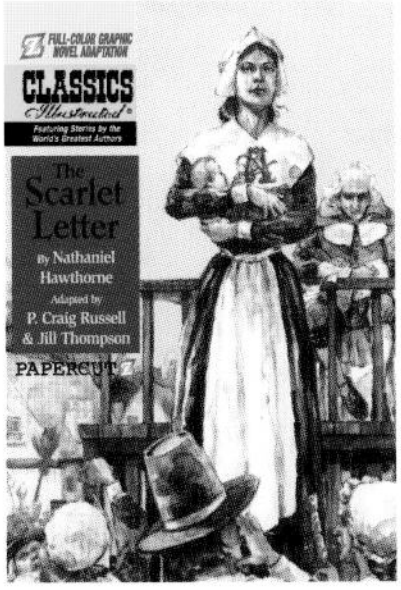
FULL-COLOR GRAPHIC NOVEL ADAPTATION
CLASSICS Illustrated
The Scarlet Letter
By Nathaniel Hawthorne
Adapted by
P. Craig Russell
& Jill Thompson
PAPERCUTZ

And as much as we love Nancy Drew, we at Papercutz actually publish other graphic novels you might enjoy as well! There's THE HARDY BOYS, of course! And Tinker Bell stars in the DISNEY FAIRIES graphic novels. If sci-fi action appeals to you, we suggest BIONICLE graphic novels based on the LEGO constructible action figures. For fun-filled adventure, you can't beat the GERONIMO STILTON graphic novels. But in the spirit of NANCY DREW "Vampire Hunter," we suggest you check out "The Scarlet Letter," a comics adaptation of the Nathaniel Hawthorne novel by P. Craig Russell and Jill Thompson. While the Scarlet Letter is a far more serious story than "Vampire Hunter," both stories feature a character that is misjudged by others. On the following pages, we're presenting an excerpt from the CLASSICS ILLUSTRATED Graphic Novel #6 "The Scarlet Letter." We hope you enjoy it. For information on other CLASSICS ILLUSTRATED titles, and everything else Papercutz is up to, visit www.papercutz.com.

Let us know what you think of this graphic novel—write to us at Nancy Drew c/o PAPERCUTZ, 40 Exchange Place, Suite 1308, New York, NY 10005 or send an email to me at salicrup@papercutz.com. We love hearing what you think, and appreciate any thoughts, comments, and even criticisms you may have. Don't be shy—write to Papercutz and let your voice be heard!

Until we meet again, keep sleuthing!

Thanks,

Jim

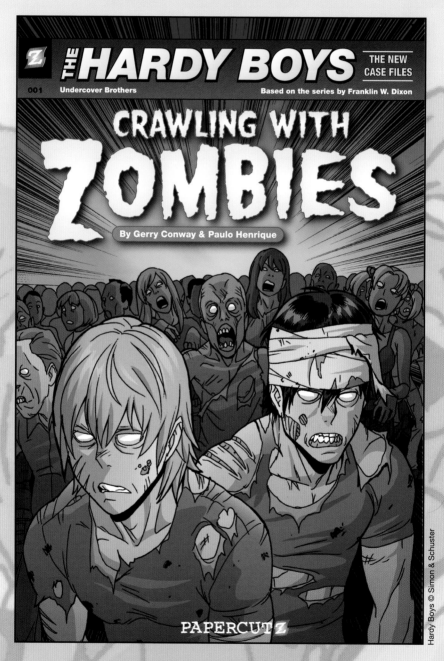

Special excerpt of CLASSICS ILLUSTRATED Graphic Novel #6 "The Scarlet Letter"!

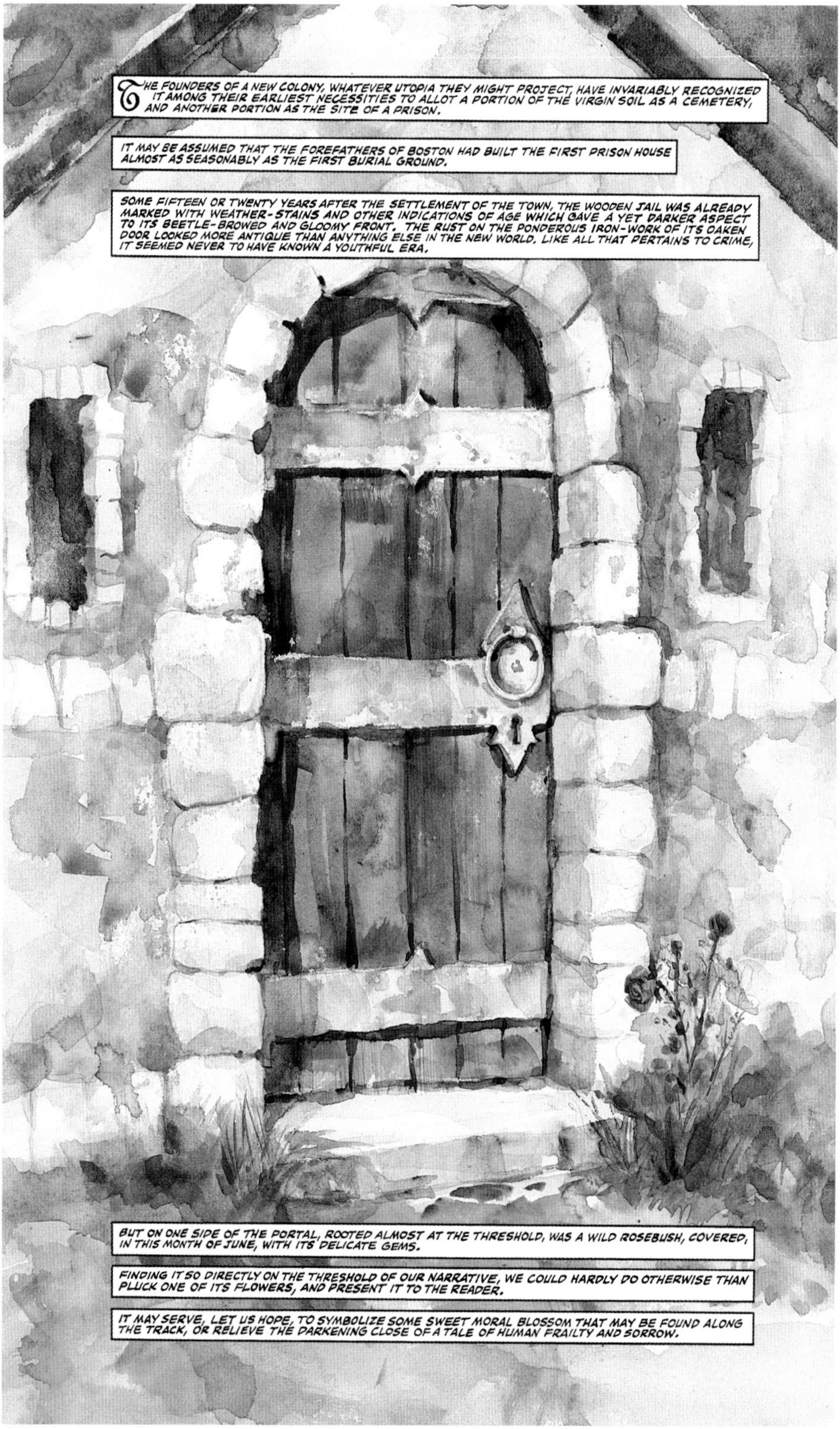
THE FOUNDERS OF A NEW COLONY, WHATEVER UTOPIA THEY MIGHT PROJECT, HAVE INVARIABLY RECOGNIZED IT AMONG THEIR EARLIEST NECESSITIES TO ALLOT A PORTION OF THE VIRGIN SOIL AS A CEMETERY, AND ANOTHER PORTION AS THE SITE OF A PRISON.
IT MAY BE ASSUMED THAT THE FOREFATHERS OF BOSTON HAD BUILT THE FIRST PRISON HOUSE ALMOST AS SEASONABLY AS THE FIRST BURIAL GROUND.
SOME FIFTEEN OR TWENTY YEARS AFTER THE SETTLEMENT OF THE TOWN, THE WOODEN JAIL WAS ALREADY MARKED WITH WEATHER-STAINS AND OTHER INDICATIONS OF AGE WHICH GAVE A YET DARKER ASPECT TO ITS BEETLE-BROWED AND GLOOMY FRONT. THE RUST ON THE PONDEROUS IRON-WORK OF ITS OAKEN DOOR LOOKED MORE ANTIQUE THAN ANYTHING ELSE IN THE NEW WORLD. LIKE ALL THAT PERTAINS TO CRIME, IT SEEMED NEVER TO HAVE KNOWN A YOUTHFUL ERA.
BUT ON ONE SIDE OF THE PORTAL, ROOTED ALMOST AT THE THRESHOLD, WAS A WILD ROSEBUSH, COVERED, IN THIS MONTH OF JUNE, WITH ITS DELICATE GEMS.
FINDING IT SO DIRECTLY ON THE THRESHOLD OF OUR NARRATIVE, WE COULD HARDLY DO OTHERWISE THAN PLUCK ONE OF ITS FLOWERS, AND PRESENT IT TO THE READER.
IT MAY SERVE, LET US HOPE, TO SYMBOLIZE SOME SWEET MORAL BLOSSOM THAT MAY BE FOUND ALONG THE TRACK, OR RELIEVE THE DARKENING CLOSE OF A TALE OF HUMAN FRAILTY AND SORROW.

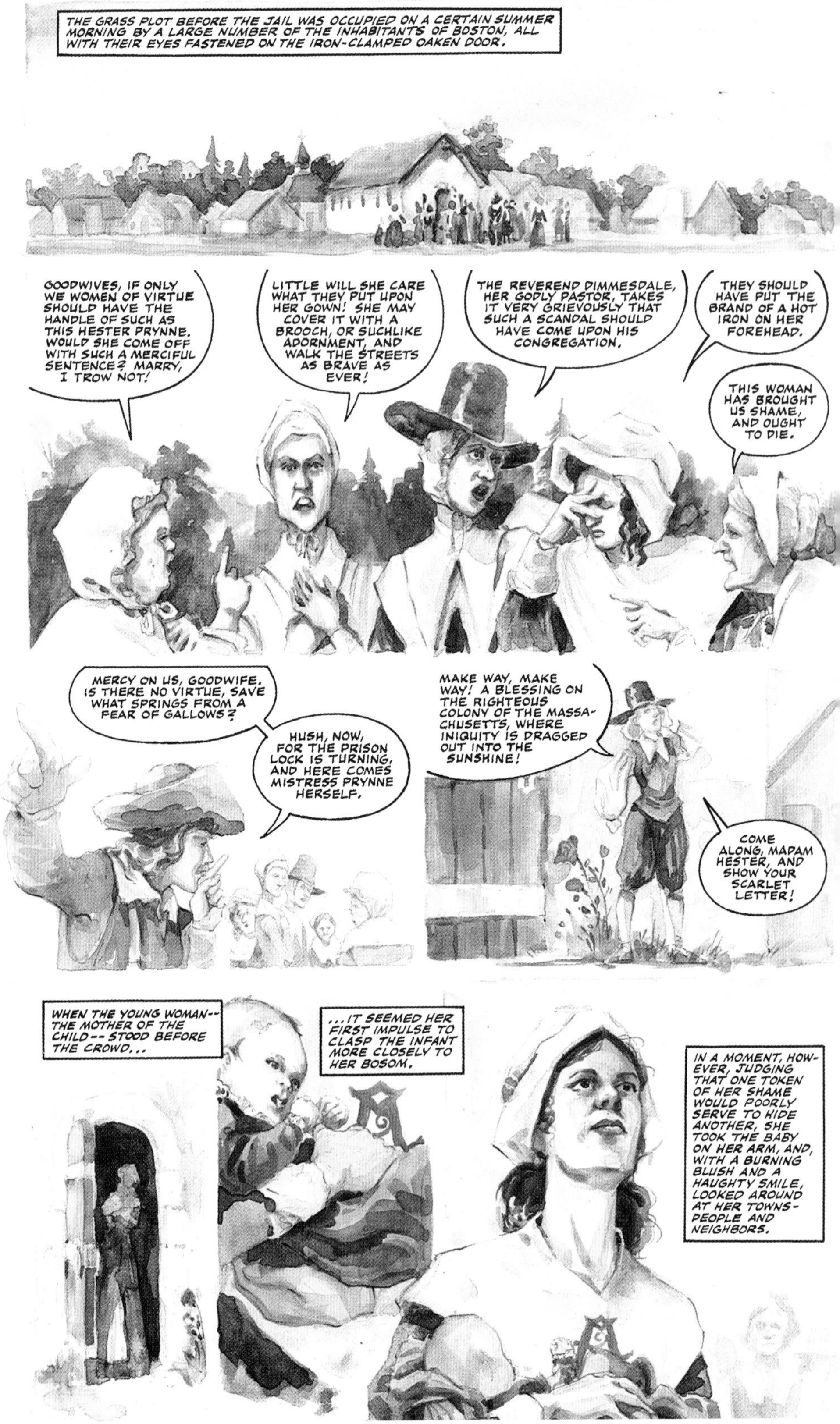
THE GRASS PLOT BEFORE THE JAIL WAS OCCUPIED ON A CERTAIN SUMMER MORNING BY A LARGE NUMBER OF THE INHABITANTS OF BOSTON, ALL WITH THEIR EYES FASTENED ON THE IRON-CLAMPED OAKEN DOOR.
GOODWIVES, IF ONLY WE WOMEN OF VIRTUE SHOULD HAVE THE HANDLE OF SUCH AS THIS HESTER PRYNNE. WOULD SHE COME OFF WITH SUCH A MERCIFUL SENTENCE? MARRY, I TROW NOT!
LITTLE WILL SHE CARE WHAT THEY PUT UPON HER GOWN! SHE MAY COVER IT WITH A BROOCH, OR SUCHLIKE ADORNMENT, AND WALK THE STREETS AS BRAVE AS EVER!
THE REVEREND DIMMESDALE, HER GODLY PASTOR, TAKES IT VERY GRIEVOUSLY THAT SUCH A SCANDAL SHOULD HAVE COME UPON HIS CONGREGATION.
THEY SHOULD HAVE PUT THE BRAND OF A HOT IRON ON HER FOREHEAD.
THIS WOMAN HAS BROUGHT US SHAME, AND OUGHT TO DIE.
MERCY ON US, GOODWIFE. IS THERE NO VIRTUE, SAVE WHAT SPRINGS FROM A FEAR OF GALLOWS?
HUSH, NOW, FOR THE PRISON LOCK IS TURNING, AND HERE COMES MISTRESS PRYNNE HERSELF.
MAKE WAY, MAKE WAY! A BLESSING ON THE RIGHTEOUS COLONY OF THE MASSACHUSETTS, WHERE INIQUITY IS DRAGGED OUT INTO THE SUNSHINE!
COME ALONG, MADAM HESTER, AND SHOW YOUR SCARLET LETTER!
WHEN THE YOUNG WOMAN-- THE MOTHER OF THE CHILD-- STOOD BEFORE THE CROWD...
...IT SEEMED HER FIRST IMPULSE TO CLASP THE INFANT MORE CLOSELY TO HER BOSOM.
IN A MOMENT, HOWEVER, JUDGING THAT ONE TOKEN OF HER SHAME WOULD POORLY SERVE TO HIDE ANOTHER, SHE TOOK THE BABY ON HER ARM, AND, WITH A BURNING BLUSH AND A HAUGHTY SMILE, LOOKED AROUND AT HER TOWNSPEOPLE AND NEIGHBORS.

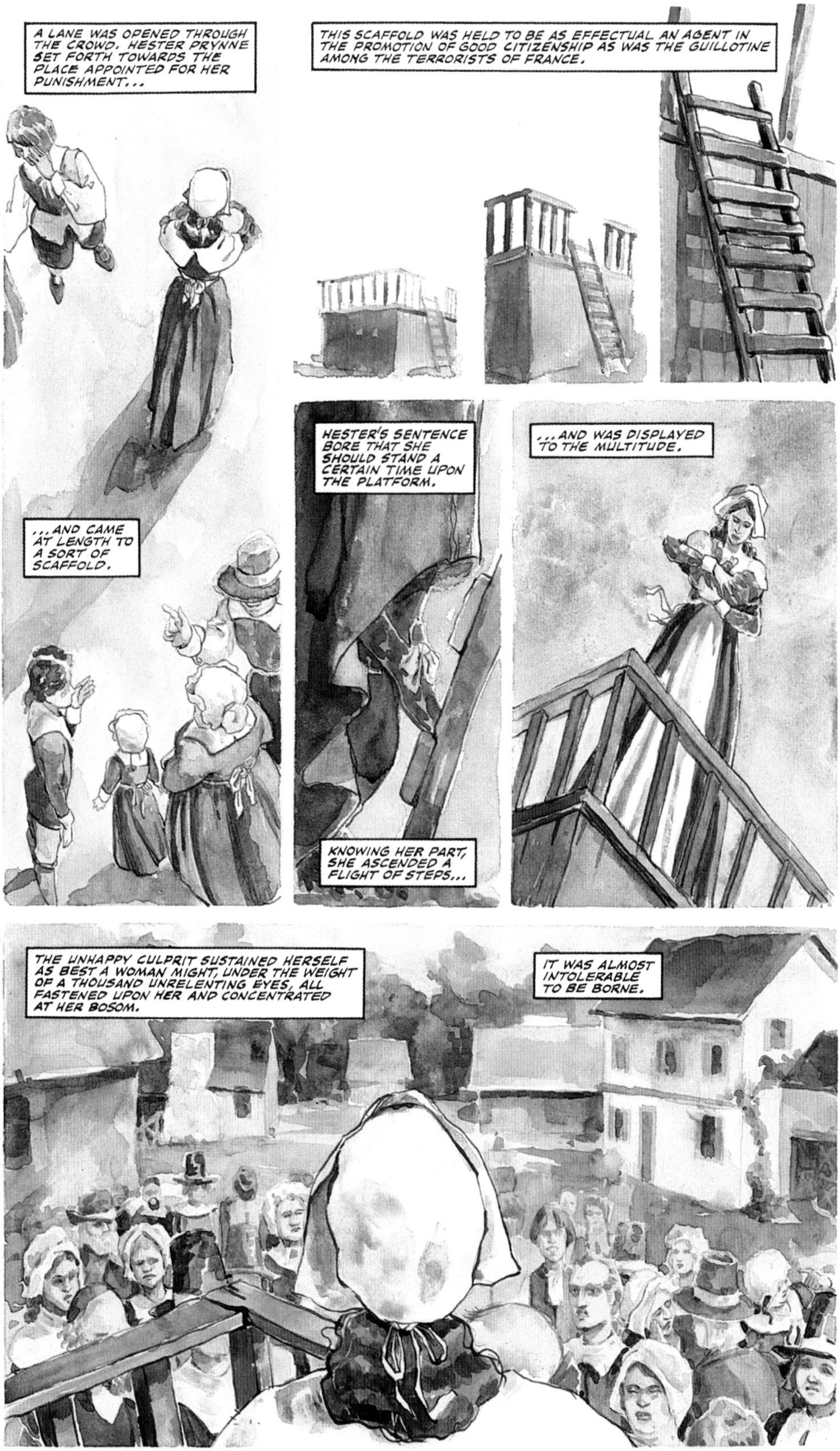

A LANE WAS OPENED THROUGH THE CROWD. HESTER PRYNNE SET FORTH TOWARDS THE PLACE APPOINTED FOR HER PUNISHMENT...
...AND CAME AT LENGTH TO A SORT OF SCAFFOLD.
THIS SCAFFOLD WAS HELD TO BE AS EFFECTUAL AN AGENT IN THE PROMOTION OF GOOD CITIZENSHIP AS WAS THE GUILLOTINE AMONG THE TERRORISTS OF FRANCE.
HESTER'S SENTENCE BORE THAT SHE SHOULD STAND A CERTAIN TIME UPON THE PLATFORM.
KNOWING HER PART, SHE ASCENDED A FLIGHT OF STEPS...
...AND WAS DISPLAYED TO THE MULTITUDE.
THE UNHAPPY CULPRIT SUSTAINED HERSELF AS BEST A WOMAN MIGHT, UNDER THE WEIGHT OF A THOUSAND UNRELENTING EYES, ALL FASTENED UPON HER AND CONCENTRATED AT HER BOSOM.
IT WAS ALMOST INTOLERABLE TO BE BORNE.

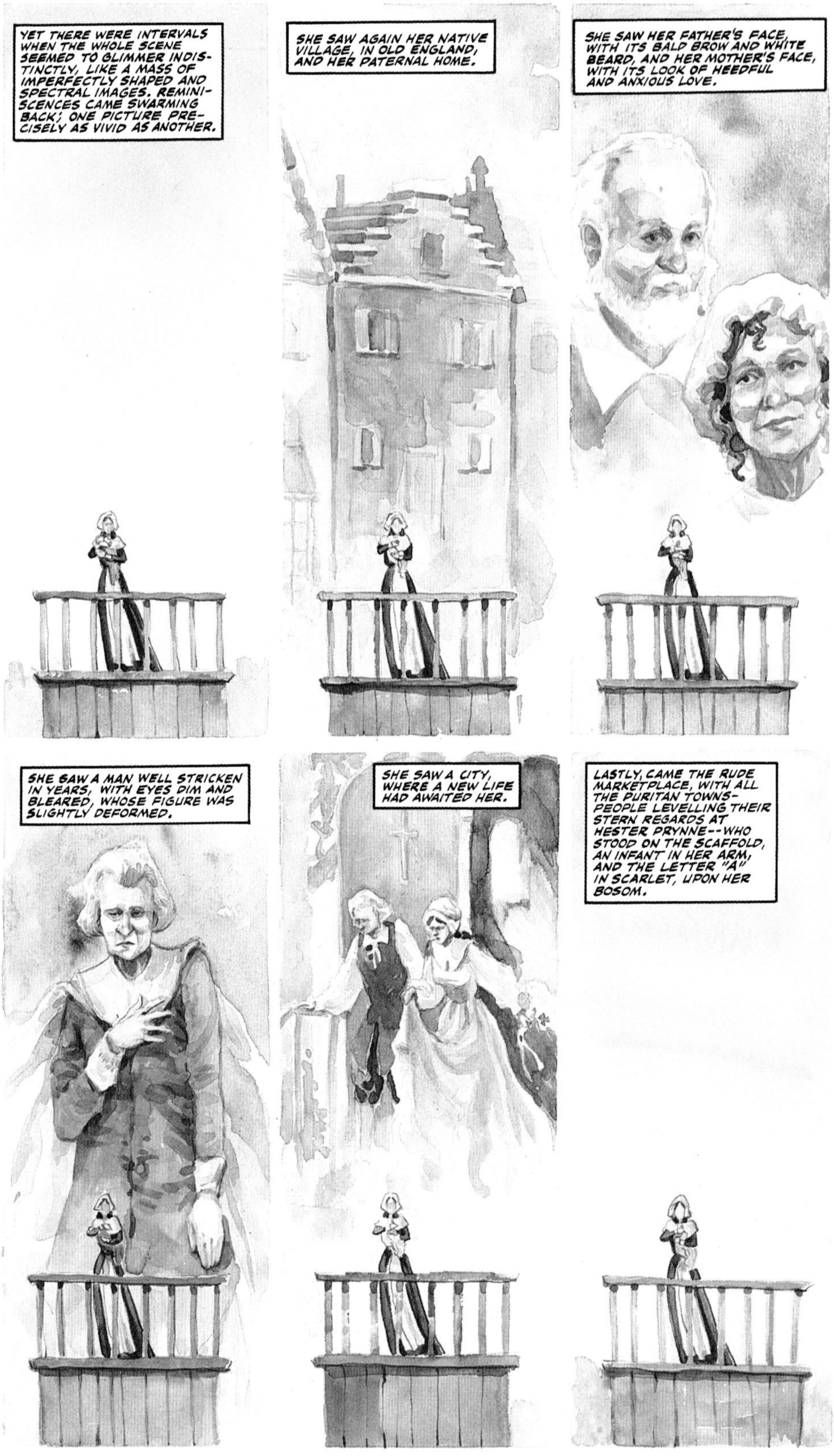
YET THERE WERE INTERVALS WHEN THE WHOLE SCENE SEEMED TO GLIMMER INDISTINCTLY, LIKE A MASS OF IMPERFECTLY SHAPED AND SPECTRAL IMAGES. REMINISCENCES CAME SWARMING BACK; ONE PICTURE PRECISELY AS VIVID AS ANOTHER.
SHE SAW AGAIN HER NATIVE VILLAGE, IN OLD ENGLAND, AND HER PATERNAL HOME.
SHE SAW HER FATHER'S FACE, WITH ITS BALD BROW AND WHITE BEARD, AND HER MOTHER'S FACE, WITH ITS LOOK OF HEEDFUL AND ANXIOUS LOVE.
SHE SAW A MAN WELL STRICKEN IN YEARS, WITH EYES DIM AND BLEARED, WHOSE FIGURE WAS SLIGHTLY DEFORMED.
SHE SAW A CITY, WHERE A NEW LIFE HAD AWAITED HER.
LASTLY, CAME THE RUDE MARKETPLACE, WITH ALL THE PURITAN TOWNSPEOPLE LEVELLING THEIR STERN REGARDS AT HESTER PRYNNE--WHO STOOD ON THE SCAFFOLD, AN INFANT IN HER ARM, AND THE LETTER "A" IN SCARLET, UPON HER BOSOM.

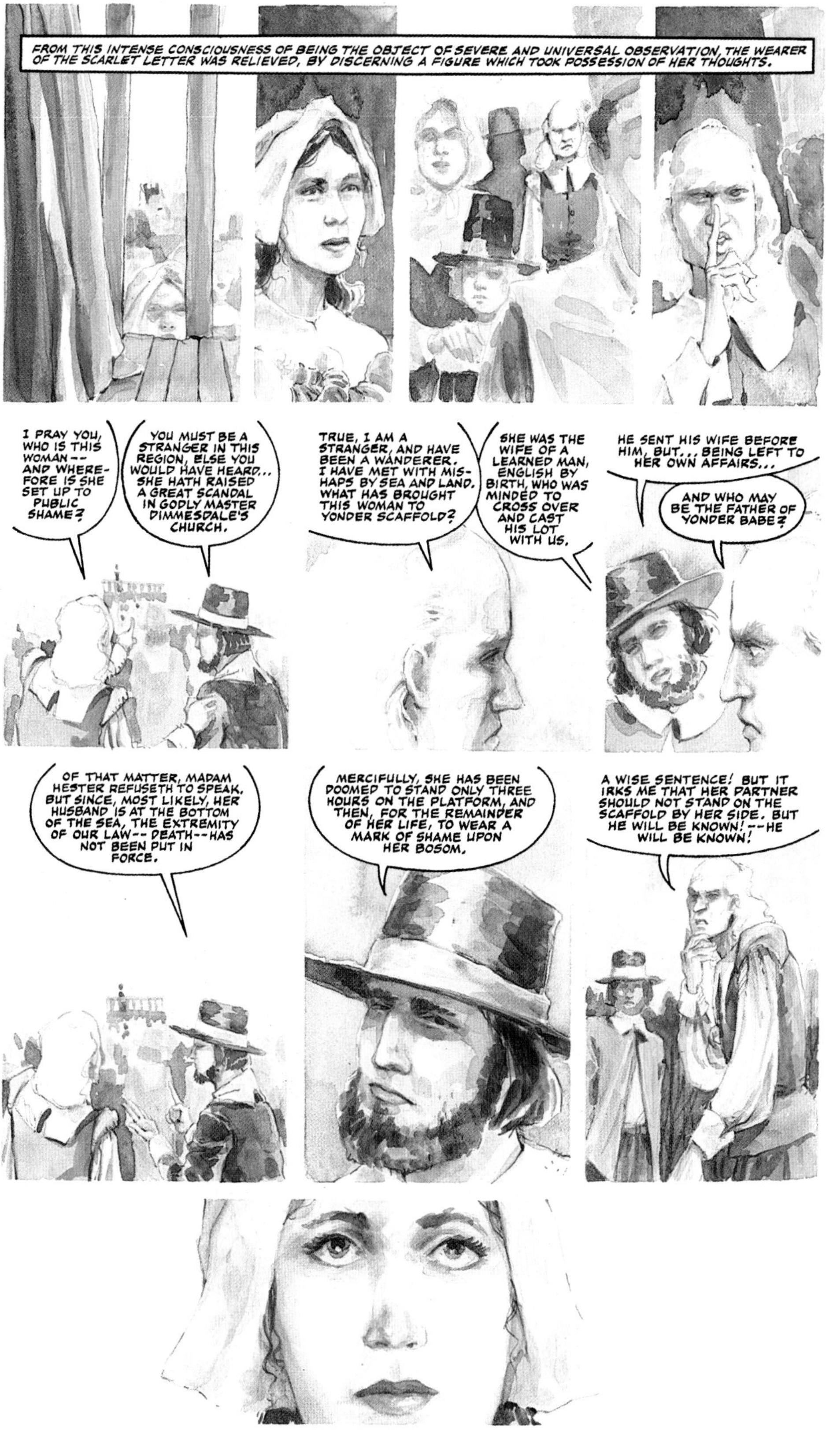
FROM THIS INTENSE CONSCIOUSNESS OF BEING THE OBJECT OF SEVERE AND UNIVERSAL OBSERVATION, THE WEARER OF THE SCARLET LETTER WAS RELIEVED, BY DISCERNING A FIGURE WHICH TOOK POSSESSION OF HER THOUGHTS.
I PRAY YOU, WHO IS THIS WOMAN-- AND WHEREFORE IS SHE SET UP TO PUBLIC SHAME?
YOU MUST BE A STRANGER IN THIS REGION, ELSE YOU WOULD HAVE HEARD... SHE HATH RAISED A GREAT SCANDAL IN GODLY MASTER DIMMESDALE'S CHURCH.
TRUE, I AM A STRANGER, AND HAVE BEEN A WANDERER. I HAVE MET WITH MISHAPS BY SEA AND LAND. WHAT HAS BROUGHT THIS WOMAN TO YONDER SCAFFOLD?
SHE WAS THE WIFE OF A LEARNED MAN, ENGLISH BY BIRTH, WHO WAS MINDED TO CROSS OVER AND CAST HIS LOT WITH US.
HE SENT HIS WIFE BEFORE HIM, BUT... BEING LEFT TO HER OWN AFFAIRS...
AND WHO MAY BE THE FATHER OF YONDER BABE?
OF THAT MATTER, MADAM HESTER REFUSETH TO SPEAK, BUT SINCE, MOST LIKELY, HER HUSBAND IS AT THE BOTTOM OF THE SEA, THE EXTREMITY OF OUR LAW-- DEATH--HAS NOT BEEN PUT IN FORCE.
MERCIFULLY, SHE HAS BEEN DOOMED TO STAND ONLY THREE HOURS ON THE PLATFORM, AND THEN, FOR THE REMAINDER OF HER LIFE, TO WEAR A MARK OF SHAME UPON HER BOSOM.
A WISE SENTENCE! BUT IT IRKS ME THAT HER PARTNER SHOULD NOT STAND ON THE SCAFFOLD BY HER SIDE. BUT HE WILL BE KNOWN! --HE WILL BE KNOWN!

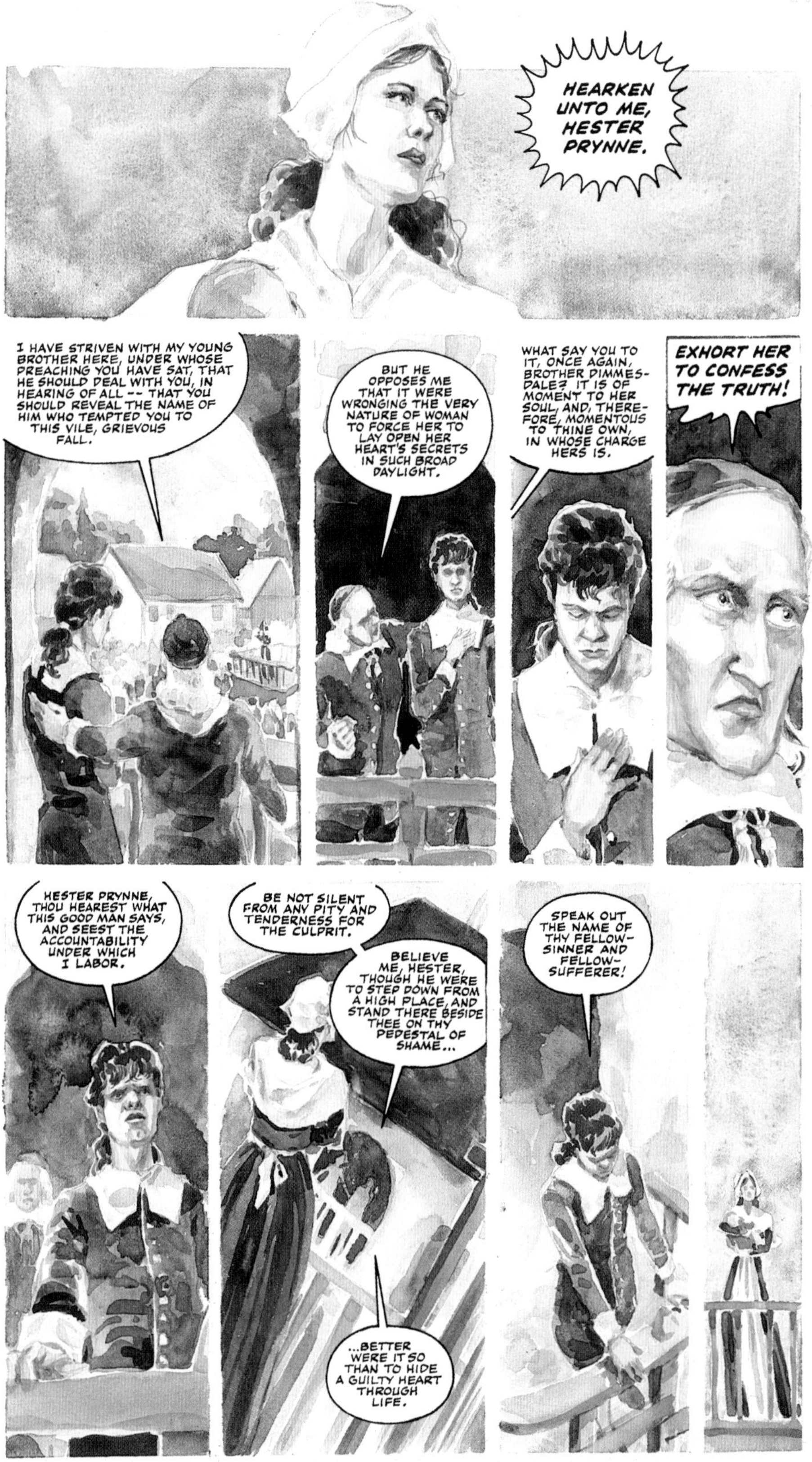
HEARKEN UNTO ME, HESTER PRYNNE.
I HAVE STRIVEN WITH MY YOUNG BROTHER HERE, UNDER WHOSE PREACHING YOU HAVE SAT, THAT HE SHOULD DEAL WITH YOU, IN HEARING OF ALL -- THAT YOU SHOULD REVEAL THE NAME OF HIM WHO TEMPTED YOU TO THIS VILE, GRIEVOUS FALL.
BUT HE OPPOSES ME THAT IT WERE WRONGING THE VERY NATURE OF WOMAN TO FORCE HER TO LAY OPEN HER HEART'S SECRETS IN SUCH BROAD DAYLIGHT.
WHAT SAY YOU TO IT, ONCE AGAIN, BROTHER DIMMESDALE? IT IS OF MOMENT TO HER SOUL, AND, THEREFORE, MOMENTOUS TO THINE OWN, IN WHOSE CHARGE HERS IS.
EXHORT HER TO CONFESS THE TRUTH!
HESTER PRYNNE, THOU HEAREST WHAT THIS GOOD MAN SAYS, AND SEEST THE ACCOUNTABILITY UNDER WHICH I LABOR.
BE NOT SILENT FROM ANY PITY AND TENDERNESS FOR THE CULPRIT.
BELIEVE ME, HESTER, THOUGH HE WERE TO STEP DOWN FROM A HIGH PLACE, AND STAND THERE BESIDE THEE ON THY PEDESTAL OF SHAME...
...BETTER WERE IT SO THAN TO HIDE A GUILTY HEART THROUGH LIFE.
SPEAK OUT THE NAME OF THY FELLOW-SINNER AND FELLOW-SUFFERER!

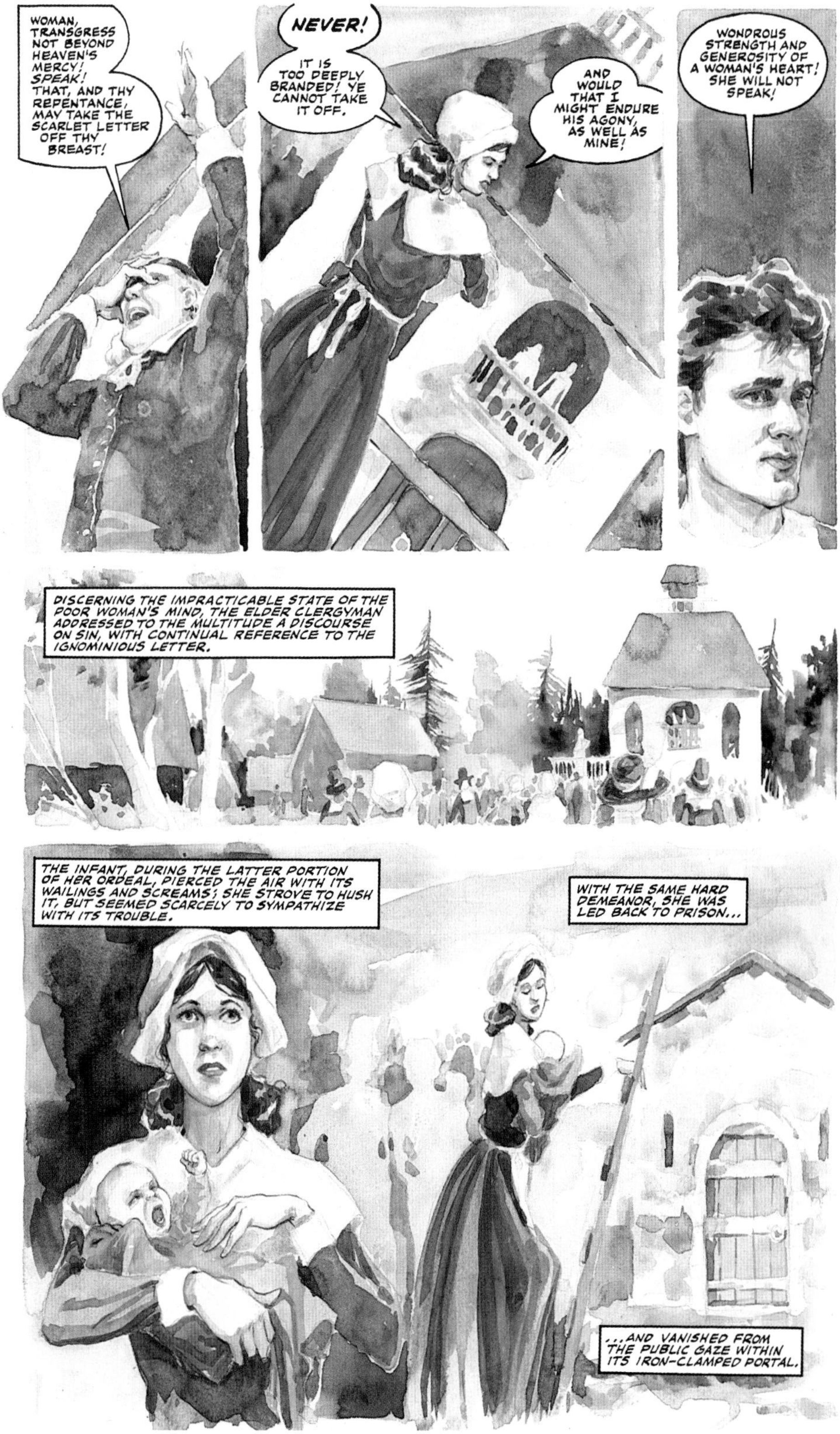
WOMAN, TRANSGRESS NOT BEYOND HEAVEN'S MERCY! SPEAK! THAT, AND THY REPENTANCE, MAY TAKE THE SCARLET LETTER OFF THY BREAST!
NEVER!
IT IS TOO DEEPLY BRANDED! YE CANNOT TAKE IT OFF.
AND WOULD THAT I MIGHT ENDURE HIS AGONY, AS WELL AS MINE!
WONDROUS STRENGTH AND GENEROSITY OF A WOMAN'S HEART! SHE WILL NOT SPEAK!
DISCERNING THE IMPRACTICABLE STATE OF THE POOR WOMAN'S MIND, THE ELDER CLERGYMAN ADDRESSED TO THE MULTITUDE A DISCOURSE ON SIN, WITH CONTINUAL REFERENCE TO THE IGNOMINIOUS LETTER.
THE INFANT, DURING THE LATTER PORTION OF HER ORDEAL, PIERCED THE AIR WITH ITS WAILINGS AND SCREAMS; SHE STROVE TO HUSH IT, BUT SEEMED SCARCELY TO SYMPATHIZE WITH ITS TROUBLE.
WITH THE SAME HARD DEMEANOR, SHE WAS LED BACK TO PRISON...
...AND VANISHED FROM THE PUBLIC GAZE WITHIN ITS IRON-CLAMPED PORTAL.

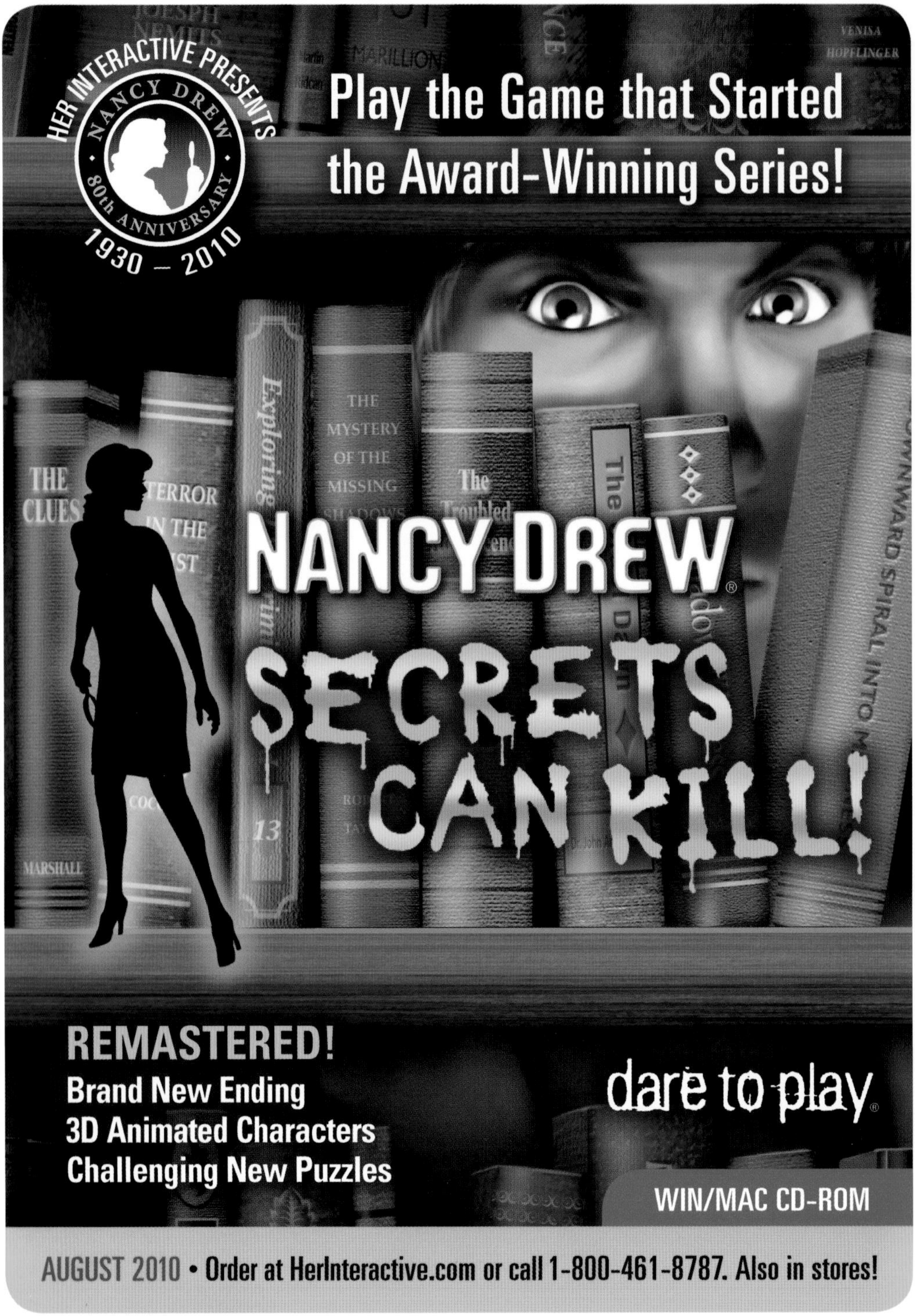

HER INTERACTIVE PRESENTS
NANCY DREW 80th ANNIVERSARY 1930 – 2010
Play the Game that Started the Award-Winning Series!
NANCY DREW®
SECRETS CAN KILL!
REMASTERED!
Brand New Ending
3D Animated Characters
Challenging New Puzzles
dare to play®
WIN/MAC CD-ROM
AUGUST 2010 • Order at HerInteractive.com or call 1-800-461-8787. Also in stores!